PRAISE FOR

"*Stephen Mertz is a Grandmaster of action/adventure!*"
—MensAdventureMagazine&Books.com

"*Stephen Mertz is the best action writer I've read in a long time . . . the Cody's War series is filled with everything you want from a master writer!*"
—Brent Towns, bestselling author of the *Team Reaper* series

"*One of the best writers in the genre!*"
—Max Allan Collins

"*The cleanest, strongest prose in the business!*"
—Gravetapping.com

"*Hard-edged . . . for those who like their tales straight and sharp!*"
—Joe R. Lansdale

"*One of the best adventure writers of our time!*"
—James M. Reasoner

"*Action-driven!*"
—Publisher's Weekly

AFGHANISTAN PAYBACK

CODY'S WAR BOOK NINE

STEPHEN MERTZ

**ROUGH
EDGES
PRESS**

ROUGH
EDGES
PRESS

Published in the United States by Wolfpack Publishing, Las Vegas

Rough Edges Press

An Imprint of Wolfpack Publishing

5130 S. Fort Apache Rd. 215-380

Las Vegas, NV 89148

roughedgespress.com

Paperback ISBN 978-1-68549-078-2

eBook ISBN 978-1-68549-077-5

LCCN 2022936145

AFGHANISTAN PAYBACK

CHAPTER 1

Afghanistan. 24 August 2021.

"Kilo-One, this is Echo-Six! We are forty kilometers out and losing altitude! Fast! I am about to make an emergency landing!"

Lieutenant Kendra Watson, USMC, clicked off-line and wrestled the stick of the Bell Super Huey chopper, narrowly missing the fireball of a surface-to-air missile streaking past. She watched it plunge skyward on a plume of smoke, still seeking them.

Damn! she thought. *Those Talis really want us gone!*

Her bird had taken a direct hit, her cargo of servicemen at risk. And her co-pilot?

She glanced at her co-pilot, Lt. Stefanie Wendell. And fought a depth-charge of despair.

A blackened hole in the thigh of Stef's flight suit was gouting blood – an unlucky shot from some Taliban keener who'd fired his AK skyward, eager to make his bones on the departing Americans being evacuated as part of Operation WHIRL-WIND, the lightning-fast US withdrawal from in-country.

Watson and Wendell could not have been more different. Tough, street-wise black Kendra and the bookish, white Stef from New Hampshire, grad student and librarian, had forged a strong working partnership and valued friendship, despite their cultural differences.

In addition to herself and Wendell, there were three in the back, Marines and Army, Now, only forty kilometers out from Kandahar Airbase, they had come under attack, their tail rotor shot out.

"Echo-Si...is your...posit—?"

The radio signal died in a scream of static.

Watson scanned the terrain ahead. The rocks below were intercut with patches of bare sand, a long, thin strip of which narrowed toward a V where two ridges came together. The rounds were whizzing up from behind them now, which meant that if she could pull off this landing they would be in a defensible position and able to hang in there until a rescue mission arrived.

"Our position is Sector Kilo-Charlie, grid A-7!" Watson said into the radio. "Going down *now!*"

The Huey, its tail rotor shot out, was hurt and shuddering through every stage of descent like a drunk with a bad case of the DTs. The nose rose sharply, rotors tilting back and blasting up a blizzard of sand that swallowed them. Watson belly breathed as she had been taught in jiu-jitsu, moving her weight into her hips and jockeying the stick. The Huey straightened, nose descending as she lowered it into the blizzard. Stones pelted the windshield. The rotors and engine shrieked. With a final forward jerk, the chopper hit with a loud *bang!* and Watson hit the emergency rotor shut-off just as the chopper plunged nose-first into the sand with bone-jarring impact.

"Everybody out!" Watson shouted.

McKnight and Showalter, both Marines, complied at once.

Davis, the Army corpsman, lingered.

He said, "You're gonna need help with Wendell, LT! Bullet hit an artery! She needs to be stabilized!"

Watson drew in a fresh lungful of breath to cuss him out, then calmed herself. Wendell's lap was coated in blood. Her hands were slack on the controls and the color had drained from her face. So, as pilot Watson made a quick decision. And, given her loyalty to Stef, an easy one.

"Do it!" she snapped.

Davis lunged forward and began tending to Wendell as Watson drew her Colt .45 from its thigh holster and stepped down from the hatch to the sand.

The voices of their attackers could already be heard approaching in the distance. They were coming, alright, and were thirsty for American blood. As ranking officer, Watson was damned if she wasn't going to make every drop cost them dearly. She approached McKnight, who stood guard with his M27 as Showalter furiously attacked the sand by the Huey's skid with his entrenching tool to build them a foxhole.

"McKnight! Report!"

"They're up behind that ridge, LT," he said, pointing. "Near as I can make out there's about two dozen. They're taking their time, but definitely headed this way."

"Okay. Stand watch. I want covering fire but hold off as long as you can and spend your rounds wisely."

"Roger that, LT."

"Showalter?" She turned to the man digging in the shadow of the Huey. "Make that wider than it is deep! Enemy's coming! Put your shoulders into it!"

"Yes, LT!" Showalter bore down and doubled his efforts. Watson stepped over him and back into the chopper.

"Davis! Report!"

A blood-spattered Davis looked up from where he knelt by Wendell. "I've applied a tourniquet, lieutenant! Haemorrhaging's stopped but she's lost a lot of blood."

Jesus! Watson clamped Wendell's shoulder and examined the mess that had once been her friend's right leg. *She's going to lose that limb,* Watson thought grimly. No doubt about it.

Just then, a hiss of radio static burst through the speakers.

"Echo-Six, this General Edwin Daniels…"

A *general?* Watson grabbed the nearest headset and grappled it to her ear.

"…have no choice but to abandon our position here. We cannot – repeat, cannot – send help at this time!"

Watson stiffened.

Operation WHIRLWIND had, like its namesake, appeared from out of nowhere. The USA and its allies had been in-country for twenty years. Twenty years of fighting, taking back street by street and village by village what the Taliban had plundered, establishing relationships with local tribesmen and rebuilding infrastructure that had nearly collapsed under the mullahs' brutal neglect. Watson and every member of her crew had lost friends in the suck. Now the brass had abruptly decided to bring everyone home. No help was on its way.

They were on their own.

Meanwhile, Daniels was winding up:

"Your sit-rep is noted and will be relayed up the chain of command. I'm...I'm sorry. God speed."

He clicked off. Watson fought a storm of rage, ready to curse out Daniels and every brass hat from here to DC and back when she caught herself and listened.

Outside, the Taliban had approached close enough for distinct voices to become distinguishable.

The time had come to fight.

"Showalter!" she cried. "How's my foxhole coming?"

"We're ready for Wendell, LT!" he called back.

She knelt. "Davis, give me a hand..."

"Begging your pardon, LT, but moving her might start the bleeding..."

"Not moving her means she buys a bullet from the Tali. Now *come on!"*

Wendell was now completely unconscious, her face white as a sheet as Watson and Davis unbuckled and lifted her from the seat. Inch by slow inch, they drew her to the edge of the hatch and eased her over into the impromptu foxhole in which McKnight and Showalter now crouched. With their help, they positioned Wendell in the deepest part of the trench. Then Watson turned to the men.

"Our guys are bugging out," she said. "No help arriving. It's just us. We're the last Americans in-country. And the bad guys are headed our way."

McKnight spat. "Screw 'em!" he cried. "Let's show 'em how we do things downtown!"

Watson grinned. "A'ight," she said, picked up a rifle and turned toward the stoney ridge. The enemy was coming.

With one final look at Stef huddled in her deep pocket of the trench, she turned her attention toward the approaching Taliban.

CHAPTER 2

When the Talis came, they came hard. And Watson and her team gave as good as they got.

The Marine Corps 'makes' Marines – that's the standard line. But in Watson's case, they had enjoyed excellent raw material. She had entered the Corps with her purple belt in BJJ and more street-fights to her credit by age 18 than most people see in a lifetime. A natural fighter, she had taken to the Corps like a duck to water. So she recognized a combative spirit when she saw one. And the Talis, however outlandish their religious and political beliefs, were born fighters. In facing them, Watson had witnessed feats of incredible valor on their part. She respected them.

The force attacking their chopper was armed with only rudimentary weapons – small arms, mostly AKs. The Russians had left a pile of them behind when they exited in '89. AKs are basically indestructible, so the Russian dump had provided fodder for many wars since. The Tali infantryman were trained.

The first wave to come at them was a line of riflemen in a direct frontal assault, bayonets fixed, firing wildly. Watson counted eight.

"Hold your fire, hold your fire," she hissed. The men's screams cut through the air, growing louder as they approached. When they were less than a hundred yards out, she screamed: "Open fire!"

As one, she, McKnight and Showalter leapt to their feet, M27s blazing. They mowed down five of the approaching Talis before the remaining three dropped prone and returned fire. As ever, Watson couldn't help but be impressed by their toughness. Rather than seek cover, they simply minimized their profiles and kept shooting.

A second wave materialized, sprinting from behind rocky cover to reinforce the first.

"LT!" McKnight waved and pointed.

Watson looked. And her heart stopped in her chest. Two of the Talis were hanging back, one spotting as the other knelt with an RPG. *If they blow the chopper, we all die right here,* she thought.

Damn it!

"Cease fire," she snapped. Her men both looked at her like she'd gone insane. But they followed suit when she threw her rifle over the edge of the foxhole and rose with her hands in the air. Surrender went against the grain of every fibre in her body, but the imperative was clear. She was in charge now, and it was her responsibility to keep the personnel under her command alive. Which wouldn't happen if that RPG opened fire.

Slowly, the Talis ceased fire. Watson breathed a sigh of relief as the man kneeling with the RPG put up the weapon and rose to his feet. The relief lasted until the first Tali to arrive grabbed the back of her head and pushed her face-first into the sand. A moment later, she felt the zap straps go around her wrists.

* * * * *

They were force-marched through the sand and scrub. The Talis had an argument over whether or not to just shoot Wendell. In the end, they improvised a sling using some branches and a blanket and forced Showalter and McKnight to carry her. Davis limped along close behind, a worried expression on his face. Watson knew her friend was unlikely to make it.

She composed her mind, drawing on every trick of self-discipline and resilience she had ever learned, and reminded herself that this little cohort of servicemen was depending on her. She was now in command and responsible for them as never before. Watson looked at each man in the face and reminded herself that each was somebody's father, somebody's brother, somebody's son. It was to those people back home that she was truly answerable. She prayed for the grace and strength not to let them down.

Their captors, the Talis that had survived the encounter, numbered fifteen. Having watched nine of their comrades die at American hands, they were less than hospitable. The pace of the march was relentless, and progress enforced by clubbing with the butts of AKs. When Davis stumbled to his knees, the

Tali closest to him stepped in and whacked him on the ear with an elbow. The bloated cauliflower on the side of his head now oozed a thin trickle of blood.

They eventually came to a road and were loaded into pickup trucks – late model Fords. No doubt gifts from the departing occupiers. The same design that made the vehicle so well suited to the terrain of Texas and New Mexico adapted perfectly to Afghanistan. *Have you driven a Ford lately?* Kendra thought, mentally reciting the old commercial jingle dug from the recesses of childhood memory. She clambered awkwardly into the truck's rear bed, hands still zip-tied behind her, supported by some rough handling by the Talis. Before long, they were jouncing down rough-hewn road to a highway pockmarked by mortar fire. They took a turn-off that ended in a fenced compound. Watson feigned a stumble as she got down from the truck. She got cuffed on the back of the head, but also got a good look through the fence. And...

Damn!

The little compound where they found themselves – just a shunt yard consisting of a half-dozen parked trucks and jeeps and some sea-cans, bordered the fence line of a huge outdoor base. It reminded Watson of Davis-Monthan Air Force Base in Tucson, the one where they keep the rows and rows of obsolete aircraft, storing them out in the desert against moisture and rust. This fenced acreage seemed comparable in size. She recognized it as a military base, but not one of hers. *Some allied force built and left this behind,* she thought. And now the Talis were using it to store captured American hardware. *The stuff we left behind,* she thought, and was amazed there was so damn much of it. In the seconds before she was hauled back to her feet, she saw jets and tanks, APCs, trucks and G-wagons. The whole shebang.

The Talis were armed to the teeth and getting set to unleash what they had on their own population and possibly those of other countries.

She and Davis were shoved toward an area of frost fencing hung with translucent plastic tarps. *A makeshift brig,* she thought. She saw McKnight and Showalter coming up behind, bearing Wendell in her improvised stretcher. Her friend was completely unconscious now, sallow and shrunken. Watson knelt beside the stretcher as it was lowered within the tarped-off rectangle of yard and the gate closed behind them. Someone secured it with a padlock and chain.

"Davis," she grated. "Fix her. That's an order."

At once, the army medic was kneeling beside Wendell. Fingers went to temples, throat, armpits and the top of the rib cage. Davis turned his head and closed his eyes, breathing, counting the beats from Wendell's heart. When he opened his eyes, they were troubled.

"Here's the sit-rep, LT. When Lieutenant Wendell was shot, she lost a lot of blood. She went unconscious, and then went into shock. That was over an hour ago. Since then, she's been losing vital functions. Her organs are shutting down one at a time. I don't have what I need to stabilize her."

"What does that mean, soldier?"

"Lieutenant, I need IV medicines, a heart monitor and an

AED. A few ampules of adrenalin."

"Okay, okay." Watson moved in beside Wendell and took her hand. "So you're telling me she's..."

"She is going to die, LT."

"McKnight." Watson spoke without turning her head. "Try to establish contact with a guard. See if you can get someone to open that gate and pay attention to us. Could be they have a clinic, medicines here. Could be they have what we need to prevent Wendell from dying."

McKnight began hammering on one of the steel gateposts with a rock, yelling and raising a racket. But it became clear after an hour that their captors were neither anywhere near, nor terribly interested in the welfare of their prisoners, even if one of them was dying. And about two hours after arriving, Lieutenant Stefanie Wendell, USMC, did exactly that.

CHAPTER 3

The present...

The chopper pilot switched on a floodlight. Illuminated in its glare was the wide circle and centered bullseye of a chopper landing pad. Jack Cody could make out the edges of a few pre-fab structures on the periphery.

"Take a look," he said to Sara Durell. "The light at the end of the tunnel."

Sara gazed in the direction he pointed. Visible through the window of the helicopter, a puddle of lights glimmered in the distance.

For the past few hours, they had been flying through pitch darkness unlit even by the moon, the rocky terrain of Uzbekistan floating by a thousand feet below the skids of their EH-60 Blackhawk Stealth helicopter. It had been a long journey to get here, hopping from airbase to airbase, to a carrier and finally to a compound of friendlies in the war-torn Ukraine. Uzbekistan was the exact opposite of 'accessible'.

They must not have much of a tourist industry, thought
Cody.

He and Sara wore desert fatigues with holstered pistols.
Cody was a top line CIA field agent. Sara was his control officer.
As lovers, theirs could at times be a complicated relationship
that had never adversely affected their job performance.

Joining them on the flight was David Kent, a relatively
young CIA officer who was acting as their native guide. With
his thick, black rimmed glasses, Polo sport shirt and beige chi-
nos, Kent looked more like a grad student than a spook. Com-
paratively new to the intelligence world, he was nevertheless
proving to be efficient, friendly and gifted in a half-dozen of
the obscure languages spoken in this part of the world. He had
been invaluable in smoothing out the obstacles they'd encountered on the way here.

"That's Tashkent up ahead," he said, his voice crackling
through the onboard radio link. "Moderate-sized city by our
standards, but the most populous in Asia. About two and a half
million people. Folks have been living there since at least the
Third Century BC. Used to be an important stop on the Silk
Road. Lotta history, here."

"Your contacts are local?" Cody asked.

"Mostly," replied Kent. "The countries in this region – Uzbekistan, Turkmenistan, the others – are a real mix of nation-
alities, religions, races. Good place to make contacts and gather
intel. The people we'll be meeting are called the National Resistance Front. Mostly Afghan, but there's also a smattering of

tribes from both sides of the border. A motley crew, but make no mistake, Mr. Cody. These are the people you want on your side if you're going to operate in this part of the world. Particularly where you're going."

"How's their level of military capability?" Sara asked.

"That varies, too, ma'am. From unit to unit," said Kent. "The NRF came together a few months before Operation WHIRL-WIND. The American evacuation lit a fire under them, driving every anti-Taliban tribe, militia and smuggling outfit under their umbrella. The one thing they all have in common is that they hate the mullahs and want to blow them to Kingdom Come. So you're going to deal with a lot of variability in tactics, professionalism and battlefield discipline."

"A motley crew, eh?" Cody said.

"You could say that." Kent nodded. "But you could do a lot worse, sir, considering."

Cody had to agree. The American departure from Afghanistan had come quickly – much faster than he and many other military men would have liked. But there were operational security issues to consider. *If the Taliban had gotten word we were heading out, they'd have dogged us every step of the way,* Cody thought. An army is at its most vulnerable in retreat. The fast bug-out had saved American lives. But the success of WHIRLWIND had created a whole new set of problems – ones Cody was here to address.

"Tell us more about our host," Sara prompted.

"General Zinoyev?" Kent nodded. "Uzbek. Muslim. He was commanding the national reserves before WHIRLWIND drove a tidal wave of Afghan dissidents to the Uzbekistan border. The government reassigned him. Now he's tasked with organizing the NRF. But understand – Uzbekistan is not *officially* involved in any of it. Zinoyev is the grease between the wheels of the Uzbek government and the Afghan field commanders that are really running the NRF on the ground in-country. He's a smart guy but has a bit of a temper. Treading lightly with him is usually a smart idea."

Cody understood. Men in Zinoyev's position were under a great deal of pressure to produce results while publicly denying involvement in the very projects they led. Zinoyev might be a grumpy type, but his support was essential to their mission. Sara, ever the diplomat, would take point with him.

While Operation WHIRLWIND was being alternately praised and derided by the press back home, there were tangible consequences to the move. US forces had been left with no choice but to abandon billions of dollars of military hardware and equipment in their haste to exit the country. In the days since, the Taliban had wasted no time in collecting, cataloguing and consolidating every tank, jet, chopper, small arm and armored personnel carrier they could lay hands on. Langley had pinpointed a base in the Panjshir Valley in eastern Afghanistan, the last holdout province in the country to fall, as the likely collection point. His mission: infiltrate the country, confirm the presence and pinpoint the location of the equipment and provide coordinates for a devastating airstrike. He would be assisted in these efforts by the NRF. Assuming all went well at the meeting with Zinoyev.

The chopper lowered itself along its beam until it touched down with a gentle bump. At the crew chief's signal, they gathered up their gear, ducked through the hatch and hustled out beneath the wash from the still-spinning rotors. The moment they were clear, the chopper began to lift off. Cody watched it rise, bank away and turn its nose toward the Ukraine. Within moments, it was gone.

Two men approached from the doorway of one of the Quonset huts. Sara and Cody turned to David Kent.

"You're up," said Cody. But he needn't have bothered. The young CIA officer had, upon stepping onto Uzbek soil, transformed from a diffident intel newbie to the life of the party. He strode up to one of the men and bellowed something in Uzbek which prompted laughter. A moment later, he and the other guy were embracing. Arms around each other's shoulders, they approached Cody and Sara.

"Mr. Cody, Ms. Durell...allow me to introduce Yurgi." A shaggy, bearded young man stepped forward, offering a handshake to Cody and a bow to Sara. "Yurgi is a Czech NRF volunteer. He'll be your main liaison with NRF forces in-country."

"Is pleasure to meet!" exclaimed Yurgi. "CIA very famous. Great honor!"

"It's nice to meet you, too." Sara smiled.

"This other gentleman is Col. Aripov." Kent offered the colonel a deferential nod. "He is General Zinoyev's chief of staff."

"It's good you are here," said Aripov, shaking hands. Cody read worry in the man's expression. "We have set up for you a briefing. Commanders from both Uzbek and NRF forces are present. And…an unexpected guest. He has caused some tension."

"What guest?" asked Sara as they approached the doorway of the nearest hut.

Tension? Cody thought. Tonight's meeting was supposed to be held in the utmost secrecy. That certainly seemed to be the mood of the half-dozen or so men grouped around the conference table in the main room as they stepped inside. Cody's quick scan identified emblems from the Uzbek and free Afghan forces. Others were dressed in the traditional rural robes of Afghan tribesmen. *Those would be the NRF ground commanders,* he thought. Their attention, like that of the Uzbek and old Afghan forces, was on a seventh uniformed man who stood apart, watching the proceedings. Sara grasped Kent's sleeve and put her lips close to his ear.

"Who invited the damn Russian?" she hissed.

CHAPTER 4

Exactly one hour before sunrise, as she had every morning for years, Shakira Nazari awoke and rolled from bed. The village around her grandmother's house was eerily still in the quiet time before the call to prayer. The young Afghan girl had dressed before crawling under the blankets the night before. Going to her knees, she reached beneath her bed and drew out a rolled bundle.

There is nothing in Islam or the Q'uran that denies me this, she reminded herself. It was fine for her to indulge this strange passion.

She was different from the other girls. Not in any obvious way, of course. She had the same very rudimentary education, wore the same modest clothing, hovered close to the older women to learn the skills necessary for maturity and motherhood. But from the time she had been little, her passion had grown within her, nurtured in secret. Only two other people knew she still indulged it. One was Mafuz, the village blacksmith. The other was Washington, the black American serviceman who had gifted Shakira with the contents of the rolled bundle.

She unwound the cloth, exposing layer after layer of cloth concealing the treasure within.

There.

A pair of purple FuelCell RV Elite female running sneakers, laceless with the mid-sole cut-out. Corporal Washington had explained that these were the type of shoes worn by elite runners. "The kind you're going to be," he'd said. It was Corporal Washington from In-dee-anna who had spoken to her of Jesse Owens, of Zola Budd. If her love of running blazed high within her, he had poured fuel on that fire.

Shakira slipped her feet into the shoes, snuck to the door and let herself out onto the dirt street. She stretched as Washington, himself a runner, had shown her, lunging first to one side then the other, extending and stretching over the knee, swinging her hips around a few times. Then she was...*off!*

Within moment she was at the outskirts of the village, tearing past the open workshop where Mafuz, the village blacksmith, was already pouring wood onto his forge-fire for the day's work. The elderly Tajik, stripped to the waist and still powerful at age 75, looked at her and shook his head in doleful amusement as she streaked past.

"Girl, you should have a male escort!" he chided her.

"I know, grandfather, but no man can keep up with *meeeeeeee!*"

Her laughter and her footfalls echoed through the rolling hills and vanished. Such a strange child! The old blacksmith smirked, shook his head again and bent to his bellows.

* * * * *

She had always run.

The only education available in her nameless village was the *madrassa*. Run by the mullah, its curriculum had centered around dreary repetition and recitation of Q'uranic verses. Girls were permitted to attend up to age nine. Afterwards, it was boys only.

But the mullah had been a wise man, and a compassionate one. He had known that children were not meant to remain cooped up in a room for endless hours. At the school day's mid-point, he would lead them out into the yard and encourage them to exercise, to run and play. This was unusual among men who taught *madrassa,* but the villagers tolerated the mullah's eccentricities and progressive ideas, for he had taught generations of their children, and none were the worse for it.

The footraces had begun spontaneously. Boys challenged each other, and the old mullah encouraged this peaceful competition. Sorting out the fast from the slow and the strong from the weak, he claimed, was important in life. And so when Shakira had challenged the fastest boy, the mullah had been supportive. It was good, he said, for each to learn their place. And so he had refereed the race himself. And appeared only slightly embarrassed when Shakira left the class champion in the dust.

From then on, she had been known as the Girl Who Runs. Viewed as eccentric by most of the villagers, her prowess was nevertheless respected and praised, even among the men. It was agreed among the village elders that should disaster ever befall them and a messenger be needed to speed word of their distress to the outside world, that task should be Shakira's. The elders' council had grudgingly agreed. And the attending grandmothers had smiled quietly to each other.

* * * * *

And so Shakira saw herself as having two jobs. The first was to give children to her fiancé once they were married. And the second was to maintain her capabilities as a runner in case they were ever needed by the village.

And so she had taken to running each morning, the tough soles of her bare feet becoming callused by the rocky roads around their village. Her path had taken her one morning past a lone American sitting guard on the fender of a Humvee, and so Corporal Washington had entered her life.

Washington explained to her that running was a sport held in high esteem all over the world. That there were traditions of exercise and conditioning, diet and mental training that went into doing it well. He explained that the right footwear would prolong her time in the sport and make her faster. He had shown her photos from his editions of *Runner's World* magazine, had brightened her heart with the story of Jesse Owens' victory in the Berlin Olympics.

"Perhaps one day you'll run in the Olympics," he'd suggested.

Perhaps. But honing her talent for the benefit of her village was reason enough for her to accept the gift of shoes, to learn all Washington had had to share and continue to come out and run each morning as hard as she could to the fence of the abandoned base left by the French.

Only this morning, it wasn't abandoned.

Shakira rounded the corner between the sand dunes at the top of the road and skidded to a stop. She stood exposed for two full breaths before diving for cover.

Overnight, the base had become filled. Every square inch of empty space was now crowded with vehicles – trucks and tanks. And movement. There were *people* below...

She poked her head around the edge of the dune and squinted.

There were four – no, *five* – of them. All contained in a fenced square, secured by chain lock and hung with translucent plastic. Four were erect and mobile while the fifth lay prone. Shakira closed her eyes and listened. Recognized English.

Prisoners!

There could be no other explanation. The Allies had abandoned the country. Everyone knew this. So if anyone was speaking English, it was because they had been left behind and captured. She thought on all this as she ran back.

Mafuz did not just live on the edge of their village because of his noxious fires and clanging work at all hours of the day and night. He was also something of an eccentric – an outsider who had learned some French and become acquainted with the westerners at the base. Mafuz, who was rumored to have hosted men of the Alliance in his home as friends and might even possibly remain in touch with some of them. Shakira took a chance and decided to trust him.

She skidded to a stop beside his forge.

"Mafuz," she said. "The Pashtu have taken the base. They are collecting all the weapons the Allies left behind. And there are prisoners. English. I saw and heard with my own eyes and ears."

"How many prisoners?" he asked calmly.

"Five."

He nodded. Watched the strange girl as she ran home. When she was out of sight, he bent and retrieved a wrapped bundle from his workbench. Unrolling it, he lifted a cellphone from its folds, punched a key and held it to his ear. A moment later he began whispering urgently in French.

CHAPTER 5

"Who invited the damn Russian?"

Yurgi and Kent exchanged a glance, then turned to Sara. Neither seemed terribly eager to answer her question. Cody, meanwhile, studied the Russian military officer who stood examining them with an expression of amusement on his aquiline features. He had the burnished skin and slightly Oriental features of the Mongol. Cody recognized the rank insignia on his uniform as belonging to a Colonel but could make nothing of the remaining insignia. The combat boots were clean but worn. He wore a sidearm in a holster that showed similar signs of use. And he held his lean, rangy physique with a calm kind of confidence. He was a tough mother, no doubt. *This guy's a field commander, not a desk jockey,* Cody thought. That much was obvious.

At the table were six men. The one who sat roughly at their center, the one beside whom Aripov had positioned himself and was doubtless Zinoyev, spoke up sharply. Kent translated his words:

"I hope to discuss strategy, the general is saying." Kent frowned. "Instead, he says, he is hosting a summit meeting between America and Russia. He claims neither one cares about the Afghan people."

At this, the Russian officer raised his chin and snapped back in Uzbek. "The Russian Colonel's name is Markov," Kent continued. "Markov says the Soviet Union more than proved its concern for the welfare of Afghans by the blood and treasure it spent there in the Eighties."

Zinoyev shot back.

"And where is your mighty Soviet Union now?" Kent translated as the men around the table burst out in laughter.

The Russian absorbed this all with expressionless calm. He turned and spoke to Cody and Sara in English, which Kent translated for the men at the table.

"I am Colonel Georgi Markov of the 7th Mountain Air Assault Division." He nodded instead of offering a handshake. "As you can see, General Zinoyev has a sense of humor. Our involvement with his forces and NHF is secret. As is yours. And yet he decides to host us both at once."

"We're with the US State Department," Sara lied. "We're here to coordinate aid to the NHF."

"You are Sara Durell of the CIA," said Markov boredly, settling his eyes on her. "I don't know your companion, but I assume he also is American intelligence officer. Let us put our cards on the table, like in old western cowboy movie. You are here to meet NHF. Me too. Our airborne division has been in communication with General Zinoyev."

Upon hearing his name, Zinoyev stood and made a sweeping gesture intended to invite Markov and the American guests to sit. As Cody and Sara grabbed chairs, Zinoyev embarked on what sounded like an epic rant in Uzbek. Cody glanced over at Kent, awaiting a translation. But as Zinoyev batted on, the young intelligence officer looked increasingly uncomfortable.

"He's raking the Russians and the Americans over the coals," Kent whispered finally. "Got nothing good to say about either side. He's really laying it on thick, too. Questioning the manhood of 'Christian' powers, which is how he views Russia and America. He speaks of the west moving into eclipse. He says the future will be created in the marketplaces and mosques of the East."

Cody glanced at Markov. The Russian, who apparently spoke Uzbek, took this all in stride with his characteristically bored expression. When Zinoyev wound down, his final remarks were greeted with jeering laughter by the Afghan tribal commanders. Markov resumed speaking to Cody and Sara as if he had not been interrupted.

"Our Division has been providing intelligence to the NHF," Markov said, shrugging as if to show that he considered revealing this arrangement to be no big deal. "We are mostly indifferent to the Taliban and their stupidity. But we frustrate their efforts wherever and whenever we can."

Zinoyev spoke sharply to a staffer who disappeared into a back room and returned wheeling in a large flatscreen TV. Zinoyev produced a remote, switching the TV on to reveal an aerial shot of the Afghan frontier. Cody recognized the Cyrillic timestamp to be Russian lettering.

"Seems your guy has a real sense of humor," he told Markov. "I'm guessing this is drone footage you supplied?"

Markov reacted to this with a smirk, a shrug and a settling

into his chair as if answering such questions was beneath him. By then, Kent was translating the words of one of the free Afghan forces commanders.

"Apparently, units operating in this province have reported convoys of equipment being driven to this base that was built and abandoned by French military some years ago." Kent turned to Yurgi. "You know the place?"

"I do." Yurgi turned to Cody. "Not far, if you travel by helicopter. A few days from here by foot."

"That's our base," Sara muttered to Cody. "Same one CIA identified."

"What do we know about opposition in the area?" Cody asked. Kent conveyed the question to Zinoyev, who used it as an opportunity to grandstand. Which Cody was beginning to realize was the man's preferred mode of self-expression.

"That area is still uncontrolled. Lawless," Kent translated. "If our forces were allowed to cross over and engage, it would be a different story. But the region's chaos makes it easy for other, lesser commanders to make a name for themselves. Ordinarily, there would be a provincial governor for the area. But these Taliban are lawless, barbarian assholes." (Kent nodded to Cody, underscoring that this characterization was Zinoyev's, not his own.) "The man commanding the region and the man commanding the base are probably one in the same. His name is Abdul Massoud."

He paused to see if the name sparked recognition in his guests. When it did not, he continued.

"Massoud is insane." Zinoyev glared at Cody as he said it, daring him to disagree. "It was your country that made him that way. He was one of yours. He attended school in America.

At Ay-ton."

Sara frowned until Markov spoke up.

"The school is called 'Eton' and it is in Great Britain," Markov corrected him. "Both countries speak English so I understand how confusing it must be for you." Turning to Cody and Sara, he continued. "Massoud was a rising star under the old Taliban government. They sponsored his education abroad. He was to take a senior position but then his mentor – his 'patron', if you will – got displaced in a political purge. Massoud was left, as you Americans say, to 'twist in the wind.' Something happened to him."

"What?" asked Sara.

"He went insane." Markov grimaced, showing a flicker of discomfort. "He drifted to the fringes of their movement. Still loyal to the cause, but... Erratic. The senior-most Taliban recognize his worth but refuse to promote him beyond a field commission. So he has taken to building a personality cult."

"So he's a warlord?" asked Cody.

"That is the term he uses for himself," said Markov. "He styles himself after the heroic leaders of early Islam. He even carries around a ceremonial scimitar – an ancient relic he's had sharpened and refurbished. His habit is to produce it meetings and lay it on the table to show he means business. To make a point, he sometimes lifts and brandishes it."

"All very *Thousand and One Arabian Knights,*" muttered Kent.

Markov nodded. "The sword's main function is for use in punishing those who defy Massoud..." Markov drew a finger across his throat. Cody took his meaning.

CHAPTER 6

President Martin Harwood had always been a 'lead-from-the-front' kind of guy. His preferred method of leadership – MBWA (management by walking around) – was severely crimped by the realities of White House protocol. But from habit, he kept his ear to the ground. So he noticed disquiet among the Secret Service agents in his protection detail almost immediately.

"C'mon, Chris," said the President, motioning in for Special Agent Chris Demer to step into the Oval as folks from his last meeting of the day filed out. "I know something's up with you guys. What's going on?"

Demer hesitated. He was supposed to avoid saying or doing anything to upset the Protectee. But he was also trained to respond quickly and honestly to any question. "Mr. President, we have a situation downstairs in the Blue Room. Someone –"

Demer paused, his right hand touching the earpiece of his covert radio. He listened briefly before continuing.

"We have someone who is refusing to leave, sir."

"Who? A member of the public?"

"That's the problem, sir." Demer shrugged helplessly. "He's an army general. Been showing up every day for the past three days. He's been here for hours, demanding to speak with you, sir."

"Who?"

"I'll check, sir." Demer spoke into his wrist mike. "Eagle wants to know the intruder's name." He paused before answering Harwood's question. "It's a General Edwin Daniels, sir. Just back from Afghanistan."

"Daniels?" Harwood frowned. He'd heard the name before, and in a positive light. "Wants to speak to me, eh?" Harwood pondered for a moment. "Okay, Chris. C'mon."

Harwood's meetings for the day were over. But Demer's eyebrows jumped when, instead of heading for the residence, the President made for the main entrance complex of the White House.

"Eagle is moving," Demer said into his wrist mike. Instantly, a bubble of agents appeared and surrounded the President. Harwood set a brisk pace, forcing the agents to scramble as he left the 'staff only' area of the White House and entered the public area. The last tour of the day was spiraling through under the smiling supervision of an official White House tour guide.

"...and here we see two of the portraits saved by Dolly Madison during the War of 18... My God, it's the President!"

A cluster of tourists turned as Harwood swept by. "Hi, folks," he said. "Don't mind me. Just passing through. Gotta' go talk to one of my guys."

A front-end loader would be necessary to collect all the

dropped jaws littering the marble floor as Harwood passed the tour group and entered the Blue Room, one of three entrance vestibules near the main portico. Inside, he found three Secret Service agents and a uniformed Capitol Hill policeman speaking to an agitated General Daniels who stood in full dress uniform, holding a file folder under his arm.

"General Daniels!" Harwood stepped up and put his hands on his hips. "What the hell are you doing coming in here and disrupting business in the People's House?"

"Mr. President." Daniels snapped to attention and saluted. "Sir, I come on urgent business."

"So urgent it can't follow the proper chain of command?" The President nodded to the Capitol Hill cop and the Secret Service agents. They withdrew, leaving the two men alone with only Harwood's body man hovering at the edge of the room.

"Mr. President, five of our people are being held in Afghanistan." Daniels proffered the file folder. "Marine evac chopper Echo-Six was en route to Kandahar Airbase for the bug-out when they got shot down. Sir, I spoke to the pilot personally on the radio. They survived the crash and were taken prisoner by the Taliban. The Taliban commander I spoke to said he was planning to execute them."

"Wait. You *spoke* to the Taliban commander?" Harwood took the file folder and opened it.

"Yes, sir." Harwood was breathing a little easier now, obviously glad to finally get this off his chest. "After the chopper was shot down, the Taliban commander got on the radio and replied to my message. He said he would make the execution of our men merciful."

"And what did you say?"

"I told the bastard I'd see him strung up first chance I got, sir."

"That's the right answer." The President examined the contents of the folder. The covering memo outlined the basics in point form: date, time and location of the crash, available info on the sector and its players, actions to date. "Is this the crash site, here?" He held up a digital photograph.

"Yes, sir. I had our drone guys do a flyover and snap those. As near as we can determine, the crew was removed and transported elsewhere. Intel has a few ideas on where."

"Mr. President, you have to do something!"

Harwood and the general turned. A few of members of the tour group had clustered around the doorway. The speaker, a man in thick Coke-bottle glasses with a camera looped around his neck, stood surrounded by a handful of his fellow tourists. All wore identical expressions of concern. Somehow, they had overheard what should have been a confidential talk. The Secret Service should have shooed them away but...

This is *the People's House,* Harwood reminded himself. And then a half-dozen of them were chattering at once.

"Soldiers left behind?"

"I can't believe it!"

"...shouldn't have been there in the first place..."

"Is he gonna' do anything?"

The President examined the group in the doorway. Although Presidents routinely get heckled and threatened, it's incredibly rare for them to be confronted by the public during a confidential briefing. He weighed his options. The most predictable would be to retreat through a side door with Daniels, covered by Secret Service and insulated from accountability. But Harwood had always been a lead from the front kind of guy. He approached the small group.

"Folks," he said softly. "I'm sorry you had to hear that. It's upsetting news and not the sort of thing you should expect to encounter on a visit here. Now I need to ask you not to repeat what you've just heard. The safety of these servicemen and women may depend on it. Will you do that for me?"

The group traded glances amongst themselves. And then, with unanimous agreement, signalled their intent to cooperate.

"Every one of these men and women..." He brandished the folder. "Well, they agreed to put their lives on the line for us. That is a sacred trust. And it is one that will be honored."

"But, sir..." The man in the Coke-bottle glasses spoke again. "Are you gonna' go get them?"

Harwood smiled.

"You're goddam right we're gonna' go get them, son. Come hell or high water."

He beckoned General Daniels to accompany him back to the Oval Office.

* * * * *

"Sir, the Chief of Staff needs to speak to you..."

"And I need to speak to the Chief of Staff." Harwood pulled open the Oval Office door. "Send him in."

No sooner did he and Daniels enter the room when the side

door by the Resolute desk opened and Bob Corbett, President Harwood's Chief of Staff, entered in an excited flush.

"Bob, meet General Daniels." The President settled into his chair. "We apparently have some military personnel being held by the Taliban. Why wasn't I told about this?"

"It just came up through official channels an hour ago, sir." Corbett brandished a memo. "A Marine evac chopper was shot down by the Taliban. Two Marine pilots, two Corpsmen and one Army medic were passengers."

"We know they survived the crash," Daniels said.

"We know more than that," Corbett replied. "Sir, we've just had word from our allies in French intelligence. One of their assets in country has seen them. Sir, they're alive and we have a good fix on their present position."

"Get the coordinates to General Daniels, here." The President crossed his arms. "General, get your friend with the drone to do a flyover and snap some pics. And, Bob? We'll meet in the situation room in an hour. I want full representation. Make sure someone from Joint Special Operations Command is present. We have a rescue mission to plan."

"Yes, sir."

CHAPTER 7

I'm going to kill that son-of-a-bitch, thought Lieutenant Kendra Watson.

She was standing at the rear wall of their fenced enclosure. The Talis had removed Wendell's body an hour ago, when they brought on the bucket of slop they called dinner. Watson doubted what they served would even qualify as 'food' under the Geneva Convention but it didn't matter. She didn't eat. She didn't rest. Since they took Wendell away, she had taken to just standing here, peeping out through a tear in the translucent plastic sheeting toward the large compound beyond. And that's when she first spotted him.

He was a big bastard. Leadership obviously came naturally to him, given the way his flunkeys fell all over themselves. *Must be the CO,* she thought. He looked like a Tali CO, complete with his headgear and robes. The finishing touch came in the form of a large ceremonial sword he wore at his waist. The martial artist in Watson was not impressed.

I could take him hand-to-hand, she thought. On his shoulders rested the burden of responsibility for Stefanie Wendell's death. Didn't matter that some anonymous Tali somewhere had pulled the trigger. Stef would have survived – or, at least, had a shot at survival – with proper care. Conditions here had been part of what killed her. And the man with the sword was responsible.

I'm going to kill that son-of-a-bitch, she thought again. And made plans for the next briefing.

* * * * *

Holding 'briefings' was part of Watson's strategy for keeping her team's morale afloat and depression at bay. Each day consisted of a series of structured activities: wake up, inspection, rollcall, assigned duties, briefings. While in captivity they would live like Marines, not hapless pawns. They would clean and maintain their environment, care for each other...

And plan their escape.

It's doable, she thought. *In fact, it's begging to be done.*

The Talis were much more concerned about the equipment they were marshalling than with the welfare of their prisoners. The attention Watson and company received was almost non-existent. But there was a routine. And today, they would exploit it.

The Talis tended to come into the vicinity of their cage roughly three times per day. In the morning, they brought food and sent in a kid to swap out the bucket they were given for use as a head. In the evenings, they returned and brought dinner. And a few hours after nightfall, one would do a walk-by

and check on them. Every few days, there would be a check at
midday. But that was pretty much the sum total of their contact
with their captors.

Of the four of them, Davis was the smallest. There was a
section of fencing that was loose at the rear of the enclosure.

"Tonight's the trial run," she told them at the morning briefing. "We go right after bed check."

The three men, nodding and grinning, were definitely
game. The day passed with the shared secret palpable among
them. And when darkness fell, they listened for the footsteps
of their captors. Sure enough, they heard him approach, unlock
the gate to the shunt yard where their enclosure sat and did a
circuit of the cage. Then he left, locking the compound behind
him as he did, his footsteps retreating into the night.

Watson sat quietly, counting in her head. When she reached
two hundred, she turned to the others.

"Let's go," she whispered.

The four of them moved to the rear portion of the cage.
Davis dropped to the ground and began doing heavy breathing.
Watson and the others deployed at the fence line.

"Ready?" she whispered.

Davis drew in one last breath, gave a deep exhale and nodded.

As one, Watson, Showalter and McKnight squatted, gripped
the underside of the fence and lifted. It came up, but not by
much. Davis, his width shrunk down by the exhale, was barely
able to scooch out beneath the lifted section but he managed.

"Okay," he whispered when he was clear.

Watson and the others lowered the fence and listened as
Davis moved around the shunt yard, examining the vehicles

there. As expected, he encountered no guards: the Talis were using their resources to guard the precious military equipment in the next compound. Watson was able to make his search unmolested. Eventually, he returned to the rear section.

"Okay," he whispered again. Watson, McKnight and Showalter bent and lifted. And Davis scooched back into the enclosure, his excitement obvious.

"There's a half-dozen trucks out there, LT," he told her. "Three have keys in the ignition. And one has a winch. I can hook it to the chain holding the gate together and snap it wide."

"Perfect." Watson smiled. "We go tomorrow night."

* * * * *

They waited until the footsteps faded. Then Watson gave the signal.

As they had the night before, the three Marines squatted and gripped the underside of the fence. Davis dropped, exhaled hard and nodded when he was ready. They lifted and he scooched through.

"Pack up," Watson whispered to the others. "We're bugging out. Our own private Operation WHIRLWIND."

There wasn't much to pack. They would take the plates the Talis used to serve them dinner. A few items from Stef's pockets. But the act of gathering these things up, getting ready to go – it would keep her guys focused while she listened for the sounds of Davis's progress. She heard a truck door being opened quietly. Then the clinking of a chain – not the continuous clinking of one being unwound, but the periodic clink of a chain that had been gathered and was being carried. She saw links spill to the ground when Davis spoke next, right outside the enclosure.

"We're good, LT," he whispered. "Got a hook in the end of this. Other end is wrapped around the winch of the truck. I'll start her up, put the hammer down and smash open this chain."

Apart from the point where the fence could be lifted, it was secure enough to withstand the torque from a big truck – at least for a little while. Watson felt confident the chain would smash before the other sections of the fence gave. And by then they'd be in the truck bed.

"Do it," she whispered.

She and the others positioned themselves like they were about to run a sprint. Crouched in 'ready, set' position, they would be prepared to explode through the opening the moment it appeared.

It seemed to take Davis a short eternity to secure the hook and return to the truck.

Watson bowed her head, closed her eyes and listened.

First came the roar of the engine being started. She heard gears clank and the purr of tires crossing asphalt. Then the chain, clinking, clanking, leaping off the ground...and tensing against the other clinking chain. A whine of engine, then...

SNAP!

The chain gave and the gate leapt open.

"COME ON!"

Watson sprinted through the aperture. Ahead was the covered bed of a ten-ton. With a final glance over her shoulder to ensure Showalter and McKnight were keeping pace, she leapt into the truck bed, then turned and twisted to grapple the others in. When McKnight scrambled in, she hammered on the truck bed to signal they were in. Davis gunned the engine.

Per Watson's instructions, he had left the headlights turned off. But it wasn't taking the Talis long to figure out what was going on. Watson heard distant voices raised in alarm, and the sound of distant vehicles firing up.

They're not close, she thought excitedly. *We have that small edge...*

The truck leapt forward, engine growling. Watson bounced in the cab as they gained speed. Then the engine was shrieking and *pop!* The nose hit the gate, snapped the chain and they were out onto the road.

Davis hammered the accelerator. McKnight and Showalter crowed and hammered the floorboards. And Watson smiled tiredly.

We ain't out of the woods yet, she thought. *But we've made a damn good start.*

The road flashed by beneath their wheels. Watson pushed aside the bed's rear tarp and stuck her head out. In the distance, glimmering like fireflies, were the glow of headlights. Watson considered telling Davis to pull over and fleeing across the desert on foot. But even on a single lane road with pursuers this close behind, they had more of an advantage in the truck.

Suddenly, thrumming filled the sky behind them.

Watson's heart sank in her chest. She recognized the floodlight as belonging to a chopper. *That would be one of their new Apaches,* she thought. She'd heard rumors some Afghan pilots had defected to the Taliban. Now one had a bird aloft and was chasing them.

"Showalter! McKnight! Out the back, wait in the sand!"

"But LT!"

"GO!"

The two men leapt from the truck and scrambled up the embankment and into the desert. Watson ran to the back of the cab and hammered on the wall.

"Davis! Chopper! Bug out!"

She dashed for the rear and vaulted off just as the Apache screamed in low, its chain gun booming. She hit the road, rolled and came up in a crouch.

She saw the driver's side door open.

She saw Davis put his leg out.

Then she watched the truck mushroom in a ball of blinding fire that took him.

CHAPTER 8

Cody decided to press Markov for more about Abdul Massoud.

"How connected is he to the Taliban government in Kabul?" he asked. "You say he's a warlord. But on the outs with the leadership. Is he setting himself up to become king?"

Kent translated all of this as Cody spoke for the benefit of Zinoyev and company. Cody noted how the two Afghan tribal commanders shared a look. One of them spoke up.

"Our American friend asks a question that is very much on the mind of our tribal elders," Kent translated. "I was a young fighter when the Soviets came in 1979. The elders set aside every controversy, every blood feud to unite against the Bear. It was easy in those days."

"Easy in those days," echoed the other tribesman, nodding sadly.

"The enemy of my enemy is my friend." The first tribal leader shrugged. "We were brother Pashtu, united in our love of the Q'uran and our hatred of the foreigner. Our great-grandfathers, and our great-grandfather's grandfathers fought the outlanders. All the way back to the days of Alexander the Terrible!"

"Who?" Cody's brow wrinkled.

"We call him Alexander the Great," Kent explained. "Different story on this side of the Dardanelles."

"I'll be damned," muttered Sara.

"This Massoud is a different story," the tribal commander continued. "He has killed fellow Talibani. And Pashtu! He has killed fellow Muslims. He justifies this by claiming a love of purity. He and only he is fit to be the warrior of Islam. So you ask, my friend. Will he be a king? I think his aim is to eventually replace the government in Kabul. He sees himself as a Caliph. A warlord like Saladin."

"And what do you think?" Cody asked.

"I think any man who values himself that much more highly than his fellows is deluded!" The tribal commander shook his head. "Afghanistan has just now vanquished another invader. The most powerful nation on Earth! Our priority now must be to rebuild our country. Open more *madrassas.* Have more babies. Now is not the time for conquest or dreams of grandeur. That man – any man – must put himself at the service of his people before all else."

The other tribal commander nodded in agreement. Then Zinoyev was talking.

"Massoud commands the territory around that base," he said. "If you will go into that area, you have an excellent guide in Yurgi. Although he is a Czech, he is Muslim and has good relationships with the commanders in that area."

"Do you not think you should speak to us about this first?" shot back the tribal commander. He turned to Cody. "I mean no offense, my friend. I respect your great bravery in entering our country at this time. But you are an American. How can we know that you mean the best for us?"

Sara sat forward.

"The United States has no interest in interfering in your region," she said. "But we feel a responsibility for the weaponry left behind. Weapons that could easily be used against you and your men. Cody is entering Afghanistan for the express purpose of locating and destroying those weapons. Once he completes that mission, he will leave. You have our word on it."

"We Russians know the worth of America's *word*." Markov softened this verbal first-strike with a smile. "You say you intend to destroy the arms cache. With what? An *airstrike?* Forgive me, but we Russians recall America's so-called 'precision bombing' along the Cambodian border during your Vietnam War." He turned to the tribal commanders. "Don't fall for it. This is a ruse. Their jets will come, destroy the base and then go after your forces. Your *villages.* Your people."

The first tribal commander turned doleful eyes on Markov.

"We are touched by Russia's humanitarian concern," Kent translated, struggling to keep a straight face. "You showed your deep compassion and commitment to human rights during your long and profitable stay in our country. What can we say? We trust every word that drops from your lips."

Kent paused.

"I guess that's what you might call a 'big diss' in Afghan

tribal terms," he muttered.

Markov, for his part, shrugged and turned to the free Afghan force commander. "Give America another foothold and they'll be back to stay."

At which, the commander – a young, bearded man with a mischievous face – cocked an eyebrow. "I seriously doubt it, my friend, given their haste to leave us." He turned to Cody. "If you're to operate in our region, you'll have our assistance and support."

"We, too, will support this man's entry into our tribal homelands," affirmed the tribal commander. "Yurgi, will you accept responsibility for his conduct?"

"I will," replied the young Czech.

Markov looked angrily to Zinoyev, who merely shrugged and grinned, obviously pleased at the Russian's irritation. "He goes in to fight the Taliban," the general said. "He will inflict mass damage upon their equipment and resources. How can we not support this?"

Cody kept a poker face, but inwardly felt a growing sense of triumph. They would get all the support they needed for their mission.

"We will return to our homelands via a pass in the mountains," said the tribal commander. "The first portion of the journey is by vehicle, courtesy of our host here, General Zinoyev. We cross a bridge into Afghanistan and then continue under our own power. Part of the journey will be by horseback."

"There are areas of their province only accessible by pack animal," said Kent. "Even the Russians deployed mounted cavalry during their time in-country."

"Russia continues to have the largest cavalry force in Europe," Markov stated proudly.

An uncomfortable silence fell.

"I'm sure that's very useful in the modern world," said Sara generously.

Cody stifled a chuckle.

"We will ensure you have safe passage," the tribal commander was saying. "But once your operations commence, we must withdraw. We have operational security concerns so won't be involved directly. But we will provide transport, whatever useful intelligence we have, and our medical corpsmen should you need care."

Cody understood their dilemma and realized they were offering him what they could. "I'm grateful, thank you."

"Allah be praised," said the tribesman and Zinoyev echoed him before adding his own thoughts.

"Uzbek forces must, of course, remain neutral. But we are prepared to offer air transport for quick exit from country." He turned to Sara. "We are prepared to offer a one-way flight out of country in event of emergency. We will use unmarked aircraft and go under cover of dark. A single flight only, but we will do this for you."

Sara smiled. "We appreciate it, General. Thank you."

Cody looked over at Markov. He was staring off boredly into the distance, as though these matters were of no interest to him. But Cody knew for sure the man was beaten. He and Sara had won. The mission would proceed as planned.

CHAPTER 9

Again, the next morning, Shakira ran as she usually did. The sun burned low on the horizon, a gold-orange like the embers on Mafuz's forge. The old man was bent low over his brazier, too absorbed in his projects to notice her as she sped past. Soon she was out of the village and into the hills, where vestiges of dusk lingered in the pre-dawn shadows.

Shakira ran without fear. For while these hills were lawless, they were not entirely without government of any kind. Tradition and codes of honor governed the land out here. There was a hierarchy, and rules of ownership and alliance observed even among the true lords of these hills. And the bandit chief of this region was a man named Tarak Khan.

Shakira's heart quickened and her breathing deepened as she spoke his name in her heart.

She knew the history of her land, knew the unending cycles of invasion, generation after generation, century upon century. Afghans understand the nature of shifting alliances, of the coercive power of expediency and convenience. In such shifting sands, who demonstrates honor and real concern for the common people?

Among the people of Shakira's village, a wary respect was afforded Tarak Khan and his men. The villagers offered the bandit and his men sanctuary from time to time, in return for which Khan protected their village. This occasionally involved demonstrations of real largesse. Throughout the worst period of the American war, when conflict between the occupiers and the Taliban closed roadways and fractured supply lines, it had been Khan the bandit and his men who guided pack mules through the hills, laden with kerosene and dried goods. When cholera hit the village during the Soviet war, it was the bandits who located medicines on the black market. While there might be no honor among thieves in the west, in Shakira's part of the world, it was the thieves who demonstrated honor.

Like Tarak Khan.

His name burning like a fire in her heart, she ran harder than ever.

* * * * *

There was another name known in these hills, the very mention of which brought a shudder to her heart.

Abdul Massoud.

Massoud was the most virulent strain of Talibanism. The ideology, which was a combination of strict *sharia* Islamic law and Pashtun cultural norms, was strict enough to begin with. Under Taliban rule, all forms of western entertainment, including films and representative artwork, had been banned and women been forced to conceal themselves within the restrictive *burqa*. Harsh penalties were meted out by *muhtasib*, sharia enforcers who stopped and publicly rebuked and occasionally even punished those who violated the laws of public decency. But even they took an instructive approach. Should a citizen stop and listen contritely to their admonitions, apologize and comply with all directives, no harm would befall them.

Massoud's form of Islam was terrifyingly different.

Shakira breathed deeply, pouring speed into her sneakers as she remembered.

Massoud had appointed a man to watch over their village during the American War, a man named Omar. Omar cut a ridiculous figure, a squat, pear-shaped little man who went strutting around the village with his AK strapped to his prodigious belly, his wide and watery eyes flicking back and forth in his chubby, bearded face. The impression of humor vanished when Omar explained *altariqa*, The Way.

They used to have an open market in the village. Market day was always fun – a time to socialize and appreciate what the neighbors had grown or made. One whole side street would suddenly fill up with wheelbarrows or stalls displaying goods and the atmosphere would be relaxed and convivial. So it had been for years until the day Omar strode in with his AK bouncing up and down off of his gut.

Someone was doing something – displaying something – in a way that was un-Islamic. Granted, it was only so through the harshest and most convoluted interpretation of some obscure Q'uranic texts. But a case could be made. Shakira imagined the matter being explained calmly and reasonably by some *sharia* enforcer. Any member of her village would have courteously and contritely complied. But that was not The Way.

Omar had stopped before the offending display, shown displeasure in his eyes and waited. And when the item was not immediately removed, he brought up his AK and blasted the hapless booth-keeper to Kingdom Come.

The Way meant constant vigilance – constant attention paid – to the immediate ruler. All rulers were appointed under Abdul Massoud, whose eyes saw all, showing displeasure first. And just as his subordinates paid constant attention to the expression in those eyes, so did their subordinates pay attention in turn to the expression in theirs. No words, no dogma were needed. Merely constant vigilance, immediate compliance.

The Way was fear.

Amazing how swiftly it had spread. The entire complexion of the village changed as people took to remaining inside, the barrier of closed doors insulated them from the constant, punitive gaze of Massoud's man. Market was abandoned. From henceforth, the only time the villagers interacted was at prayers. And even then, the eyes of Omar were upon them, for he lingered just outside the doorway, attentive, his eyes ever upon their *mullah,* who spoke nothing but the prayers for fear he would transgress The Way.

The Way held even God in check.

Of course, that was not its purpose, Abdul Massoud had explained to them personally one day at their mosque. He was going around the region, then, stopping in and addressing the rural people during their times at prayer to explain *altariqa,* The Way. He reminded the people that Muslims had been in power when the British came back in the 1800s. As they had been when the Russians and Americans had come in their turn. Why was Allah punishing their people this way? Were they not electing leaders who followed the dictates of Islam?

No, said Abdul Massoud. The only possible explanation was that the leaders were *not* following the Q'uran. Or, if they were, it was in name only. Holding the appearance of *halal* while not being *halal*. And so it must fall to invigilators to watch over the people and punish sternly any who transgress. The people in turn must be guided, not by the invigilators' words but by their attention.

"By paying attention to our attention, you will learn The Way," Abdul Massoud had said, projecting his attention into the crowd by his fierce glare. "Like one trains a dog. Slowly it will spread. Until it is everywhere."

And so it had worked, with Omar's gaze growing ever more powerful over their daily lives, until the last years of the war, when military priorities had demanded a shift in focus and Omar and Massoud left their lives for a time. But the shadow of The Way remained. And Shakira could not forget the hot intensity of Abdul Massoud's presence.

And so she recognized it instantly when it appeared in the valley below.

She was at a low point on the ridge above the base, peering down at the fenced area containing the English. She saw the forms of the men – only three, now – sitting on the ground within. And she saw the group of Massoudi fighters swaggering toward it. There, front and center of the approaching group, was him.

Abdul Massoud.

Strangely, she was not afraid.

"Do you know who Harriet Tubman was?" Washington had asked the day he gave her the sneakers. When she shook her head no, he'd explained. "She was a black American woman, black like me. My people were once held as slaves. Harriet Tubman, she would rescue slaves and help them run to freedom."

"Like Jesse Owens. And Zola Budd."

"Much more important," Washington had said. "When she guided the slaves to freedom, men pursued them. And she used to tell the runners: 'If you hear the dogs, keep going. If you see the torches in the woods, keep going. If there's shouting after you, keep going. Don't ever stop. Keep going. If you want a taste of freedom, keep going.' And that's my advice to you, girl. You've had a taste of freedom, now. Don't ever give up. And if they ever come after you, keep going."

Shakira thought all these things, glaring down at Abdul Massoud with contempt.

If his shadow ever returned to her life, she would run. And she would keep going. So that even if a bullet found her, she would not have forsaken that freedom.

CHAPTER 10

Watson heard them approach, heard the footsteps of several men but only one voice. *That'll be him,* she thought. The big man with the fancy sword. The one she vowed to kill.

There was no break in the translucent tarp covering the doorway in the enclosure. But the click of the lock and the rattle of chain being withdrawn were signal enough that a visit was nigh.

"Showalter, McKnight," she said. "Over here. Behind me."

The two Marines moved to the spot she indicated. Watson then put herself between them and the doorway. She would be the first one with which the big man would have to deal.

The plastic tarp was shoved aside and held by a man wearing an AK. Watson recognized the figure of the big man shouldering his way past the sentry and into the cage. She noticed the way he ducked through the entrance, exaggerating his build, and the way he smiled and stretched as he entered their enclosure, maximizing his presence by taking up maximal space.

"Come, Ali!" he cried in English. "Come in and see!"

A second man, shorter and slighter than the boss, joined the swordsman inside the cage. Bearded, he wore glasses and betrayed a nervous hesitancy around his superior.

"You see, Ali?" The big man put his hand on the bearded one's shoulder, waving toward the Marines. "They are just men. No different from us. Nothing to fear. Despite their great reputation as Marines. Even US Marines can be humbled into submission."

"Allahu ackbar," said the bearded man nervously.

"But of course, *I* am Abdul Massoud." The big man looked at Watson as he announced this, still speaking in English for their benefit. "Abdul Massoud, vanquisher of Americans. Punisher of the unrighteous. Not everyone possesses my courage."

"No one possesses your courage, O Great One," said Ali.

"So true." The big man turned from Ali and approached Watson, amusement plain on his features. "You. What is your name?"

"Watson," she snapped, glaring right back at him.

"Watson," he repeated. "I am guessing it was you who organized the escape attempt. You have the look of one driven to win. You convinced the others to make the attempt. But then, you are also responsible for the death of the man in the truck."

"The helicopter pilot is responsible for that," she said.

"He was just doing his duty," replied Massoud. "If you had done yours, your friend would still be alive."

"If I was doing my duty, you'd be dead right now," she shot back.

"You are unarmed," he pointed out.

"I don't need weapons to kill you," she replied calmly.

At this, Massoud laughed. "Fierce!" he cried. "Like a lioness! My, you *are* a remarkable woman."

"Before this is all over," she vowed, "I'm going to kill you."

"Like you killed your comrade driving the truck?" Massoud's answering smile was thin. From his smile, it was obvious that he delighted in offering little jabs when Watson wanted nothing more than to get her teeth into his flesh.

Watson said nothing, merely glanced to Showalter and McKnight who stood, tensed and awaiting her orders.

But now Massoud was laughing. He was surprisingly attractive when he smiled. Charismatic. Under different circumstances, Watson might even have found the man attractive. He was accustomed to receiving attention, even admiration. This was a man who knew how to exploit the spotlight – how to stand in its glare such that his acts of evil fell in shadow.

"Debate and philosophy are the toys of weak men," he said finally. "Do you know why, Watson? It's because debates and philosophy are what come *after* action. True change requires no words. Only those strong enough to seize the moment and exploit it for their own purposes. Don't you agree?"

"I think if someone is strong enough to 'seize the moment,' as you say, then they should be moral enough to exploit to *everyone's* benefit."

"Oh, an idealist!" he crowed. "Are you a *Christian*, Watson? Mm? Believe in turning the other cheek and forgiving your enemies?"

"I believe that the power of love triumphs over hate," she shot back. "Every time."

"Oh, such nonsense." Massoud drew his sword. "Love can only exist within a circle of protection. A family that is unsafe cannot know love. Any more than prisoners such as yourselves who are unsafe. But what exists regardless of safety or danger? What exists regardless of war or peace, law or chaos? One thing."

He flourished the blade.

"Strength."

He turned to Ali. Then, with a nod to the guards outside, he stood aside as they rushed into the enclosure, seized the man named Ali and pushed him to his knees.

"Sadly, Ali was recently appointed captain of the guards," Massoud said, approaching the man kneeling on the asphalt. "It was his responsibility to ensure you and your men were safe and secure. It was a job he failed to do. So one could say that it was really *he* who is responsible for the death of your man."

Massoud pressed the tip of the scimitar beneath Ali's chin and forced him to raise his head.

"You have failed me," he told the cowed man. "But what is worse, you have failed to keep The Way. And so you have failed Allah."

"Allah is compassionate and merciful," stammered Ali. "Please forgive me."

"Perhaps Allah will have mercy on you then," replied Massoud. "Because I will not."

With a flash, the scimitar was hauled aloft. It hovered there, blade twinkling in the sun for a long moment before it descended with a loud *whoosh!* An instant later, Ali's bearded head fell to the sand, mouth opening and closing like a fish, glasses still perched improbably upon his nose.

Massoud bent and hauled up the head by the hair.

"Be patient, Watson," he said to her. "Soon, this will be you and your men."

He tossed the head at her feet. Then he spun on his heel and departed.

Watson watched him go.

I'm going to kill that son-of-a-bitch, she thought.

CHAPTER 11

The President waited until the members of the National Security Team had filed out of the Situation Room before turning to the trio who remained behind. The Chairman of the Joint Chiefs, the CIA Director and Bob Corbett, his Chief of Staff waited, eyes on President Harwood, as the last members departed and the door closed.

"Okay," said the President. "I've got my diplomatic work cut out for me. Bob will be arranging a call with our allies in India to inform them of our near-area operation and intent to operate in their waters. Pakistan will be kept out of the loop. Meanwhile, there are a few details I want to share here where the circle is small. But first, let's review the operational plan as it stands. General?"

The Chairman of the Joint Chiefs clicked a button on a remote control beside him. One of the flatscreens across the room burst into life with a projection of the Indian subcontinent, the Arabian Sea and Bay of Bengal to either side of it, with borderlines for Afghanistan, Pakistan and Nepal visible above the northern border.

"Per your instructions, Mr. President, we have activated US Army Delta hostage rescue team. The carrier *Ronald Reagan* is currently underway from duty of the Persian Gulf. The *Reagan* will act as our staging area and onsite command and control hub for the action. Dubbed Operation REDEMPTION, it will be a lightning strike into the Panjshir Valley with the goal of securing and airlifting our POWs to safety.

"Army Delta is now staging up at Fort Benning. They'll be boarding their transport planes within the hour. The *Ronald Reagan* will be on-station in the Arabian Sea within the next five hours. Once Army Delta arrives, we've arranged for drone sweeps over the base. We have two M-9 Reapers that will provide real-time intel and stand by as back-up in the event things go sideways.

"Once we start the clock on REDEMPTION, the Army Deltas will lift off from the *Reagan* in stealth helicopters that will cross Pakistani territory under cover of darkness. They will set down here..."

The map faded to be replaced by a satellite image of Abdul Massoud's base and the surrounding valley. The Chairman identified a spot some distance from the fence line.

"Once the choppers are down and the landing zone is secured, the Deltas will hump it across this section of desert here. It's about two miles to the base. Our hope is that by then we'll have a pretty clear picture of where the Americans are being held. One portion of the team will create a diversion while the second team goes in and liberates our guys... And any other allied soldiers we may find. Once the prisoners are secured, a signal will be sent to the choppers to come in for pick-up. That's the plan, sir, in broad strokes."

"Okay." Harwood sat forward. "It's a good plan. Mr. Chairman, thanks to you and your people for setting it up. Now I'm going to throw a curve ball into the game."

The Chairman raised his eyebrows, looked to the Director and Chief-of-Staff, then took a seat.

"As the Director knows, we already have people in-country." Now it was the President's turn to use the screen. He touched a few buttons and a map projection of the Afghan/Uzbek border region jumped on-screen. "Two days ago, we dispatched two operatives – Jack Cody and Sara Durell – to Uzbekistan. Their mission is to make contact with members of the National Resistance Force, or 'NRF', that is presently engaged in an insurgency against the Taliban government in Panjshir province. The NRF is receiving clandestine funding and equipment from the Uzbek government. They'll act as matchmaker in this little romance.

"Once contact is made, Cody's job is to infiltrate his way into Panjshir province to verify that Massoud's base is being used as a collection point for the hardware we were forced to leave behind in Operation WHIRLWIND, when we evacuated our troops from in-country. Word is that Massoud has been gathering equipment for use against his own people and possibly those of other nations. Satellite and drone data would indicate that may be what's going on. Cody's job is to verify, pinpoint and communicate the coordinates of large equipment dumps back to use for an airstrike.

"Mr. Chairman, I want you to alert the skipper of the *Rea-*

gan to have his aircrews on stand-by to deliver an airstrike. Full spectrum spread. I don't want a single goddam thing on that base in working order, even the damn toilets. Scorched earth. Burn the damn place to the ground. Your Army Delta team will proceed as ordered and wait for our word to head in-country to offer close combat support and pick up Cody once he's done. Understood?"

"Yes, sir." The Chairman nodded as he scribbled notes. "Airstrike and change of mission for Delta operators."

"Any questions for me?"

"No, sir. Seems pretty straightforward," replied the Chairman. "You said Jack Cody is the man in country now?"

"That's the guy." Harwood sat back and rubbed his forehead. He was getting tired.

"Don't they call him 'Suicide' Cody, sir?" The Chairman looked a little worried.

Silence fell over the table.

"His wife and child were killed in a terrorist bombing intended for him," said the Director quietly. "We wanted to retire him right then but he insisted on remaining operational. We call him 'Suicide' Cody because he has one requirement for every mission he takes on – that it have a slim to none chance of success. With this mission, could be Cody lives up to that nickname."

The Chairman shook his head. "Panjshir province may be the most dangerous place on Earth right now," he said.

"It's about to get a hell of a lot more dangerous," said the President.

CHAPTER 12

"This is the bridge," said David Kent, leaning over the map unrolled on the table. The meeting over, the conference room was now doubling as their ad-hoc operations center for Cody's insertion into Afghanistan. "It connects the southern tip of Uzbekistan to Afghanistan. The Russians built it in 1982 to supply their forces in-country."

"The Friendship Bridge." Sara smiled thinly. She looked from Kent to Yurgi to Cody. "Ironically, the bridge across which the Soviets withdrew in 1989."

"Soviet general wait at bridge," Yurgi said. "He wait for last tank to cross, then he leave on foot."

"How very Russian," Sara muttered.

"The Americans flew out," said Cody. "I don't suppose there's much chance of us flying *in...*"

"It's really hairy, Mr. Cody," said Kent. "That region of the border is porous. You've got refugees, smugglers, regular Taliban forces and General Zinoyev's border troops. Not to mention the NHF."

"We've got reports that some of the Afghan pilots we trained on our aircraft have switched sides," Sara said. "Some of the planes and choppers guarding the skies above Afghanistan are state-of-the-art and manned by pilots that know how to use them. Quite a welcoming committee."

"So we go in the old-fashioned way." Cody sighed. "I airlift in to an RV point where I link up with NHF forces and they bring me the rest of the way in."

Yurgi pointed to a section on the Afghanistan side near the bridge. "This pass is ancient gathering point for smugglers," he said. "I go in first. Meet up with my friends in NHF. We meet you here. You ride horse?"

Cody smiled. "Yes, I ride horse," he said.

"From here by horse is few days." Yurgi shrugged. "Is nice countryside."

Cody had never heard Afghanistan described quite that way before. But Yurgi's feelings for the place were likely shared by the locals. *That would explain why they've been able to resist invasion for centuries,* he thought. Different groups of fighters united by a simple love of country had proven again and again that they could take down armies bigger, stronger and better equipped than they.

"You'll want to take care to avoid smugglers," Kent said. "They're mostly Uzbek and Pakistani. They tend to stick close to the border regions. But the further in you go, the more dangerous it gets. It's bandit country. And those bandits have real power."

"What's the relationship between them and the Taliban?" asked Sara.

"It's complicated. Like most things in Afghanistan." Kent laughed. "Look, any government in Kabul is provisional, at best. In Afghanistan, the only real politics are local. The national leaders sit atop a shaky structure of regional governors. They, in turn, sit atop a shaky structure of warlords. What the warlords can't or don't care to control is run by bandits. They're often the guys that can provide protection and services to local villages. So villagers strike deals with the bandits. They have a symbiotic relationship. It's a system that has worked for a long time."

Cody reflected on this for a long moment. He had seen similar relationships between villagers and outlaws in Chechnya and among the Ingush. Partnering with local crime lords was not unknown in intelligence circles. Smugglers often have the best sense of how to get in and out of a country without attracting notice. Thieves and fences can assist in procurement of resources or networking. Establishing a relationship with the local bandits would be a great coup.

"Who's the head bandit in this area?" he asked, touching the base with a forefinger.

"In the Panjshir Valley?" Kent shook his head. "Guy named Tarak Khan. He's pretty hard core."

Yurgi was nodding vigorously. "Very hard core, Mr. Cody," he affirmed. "From the olden school."

It took Cody a moment to unravel that Yurgi meant "old school".

"Khan has operated in that area for a decade or more," Kent was saying. "He's something of a folk hero to the villagers in the region. He's one of the bandit lords who actually cares about the villages under his control. He's supplied food and medicine, occasionally emergency services. He'll go the extra mile to help the people. He has good reasons to be highly motivated."

"So he'd be a good guy to get on our side," said Cody. Out of the corner of his eye, he noted that Sara had stepped away from the group to answer a call on her cell. "How does he feel about the Taliban?"

"Oh, he hates them," Kent said. "But nowhere near as much as he hates Americans. Our forces operated extensively in his region in the early part of the war, since the east is the Taliban's center of power. Tarak Khan and his family vowed to stay out of the fighting but that didn't matter. Afghan forces conducted sweeps under direction from our commanders. The Afghan forces were…messy. No precision strikes for those guys."

"Khan lost family?"

"Many, Mr. Cody," said Yurgi. "His brother, first, along with his entire family. And then his daughter."

"My God," said Cody.

"He blames the Americans," said Kent. "And he may have a point. But regardless, he hates us. Holds the US in total contempt. If you end up anywhere near him, I strongly suggest you avoid contact. You'll save yourself a lot of trouble."

As ever, Yurgi was nodding vigorously in agreement.

Sara finished her call and hung up. Cody saw wariness on her features as she moved up to join the conversation.

"Just got word from Langley," she said tightly, shooting a glance at Yurgi. Deciding he was trustworthy, she continued. "Apparently, the Director was in the Situation Room for a good chunk of the day. Our mission has just had a very interesting wrinkle added to it."

CHAPTER 13

Abdul Massoud sat in the open hatchway of an Apache helicopter, wiping the blood from his scimitar.

How is it that you do not fight in the way of Allah? he thought, remembering the verse from the Q'uran. *How is it that you do not fight for the oppressed among men, women and children?*

He drew a rag down one side of the blade, sopping up the last of the blood there. It had been a shame to lose Ali for the man had shown both piety and potential. But by his inattention to duty, he had endangered them all. Killing him therefore counted as an act of mercy. It was with weapons like this scimitar that ancient Islamic warriors had fought for the oppressed. And so, in modern times, as it was with ancient weapons ...

He turned the sword on his knee and examined the blood on the other side of the blade. Then he looked up at the massed ranks of tanks and helicopters filling the base around him. Modern equivalents of the sword, many times deadlier and more powerful. And yet...

Allah is eternal, Massoud thought as he bent to wipe away more of Ali's blood.

In the glory days of his youth, as a rising star among the Taliban, Massoud had had the good fortune to be chosen to attend school in the west. Before he had gone, the elders had cautioned him about the temptations he would encounter. One, a man named Pervez, had actually lived on a western university campus during his studies of engineering and had warned Abdul Massoud that many fell away from the faith upon encountering the temptations of the infidel's world.

"It is seductive, brother," Pervez had assured him. "Graven images are everywhere. Compelling art in the form of pictures and movies to distract you from seriousness of mind. Drugs in the form of cigarettes and alcohol, coffee, narcotics. And the women! Little brother, watch out for them. For there is no creature more duplicitous, more cunning and more poisonous than an infidel woman."

Massoud had traveled to England, to the fabled university at Eton and settled there. He had taken Pervez's advice to heart and created a little haven for himself in his apartment. No furnishings, no pictures on the walls, no television. It was like a humble home in his native land. When he pulled the curtains, he could almost imagine himself back in his beloved Panjshir.

And he had needed that refuge, for all had been as Pervez claimed. At the end of the school week, the young Massoud would hurry directly to the mosque after class, eschewing invitations to attend parties and happy hours, avoiding social engagements, forming no lasting attachments to anyone who was not Muslim. Upon returning home, he would discard his western clothing and slip with relief into his desert robes, absorbing himself in his studies and prayers. His weekends, spent in his bare apartment with the blinds drawn, could just as easily be in his home village as in the college town – effectively, no different from his life in Afghanistan. In so conducting himself, he had avoided all temptations.

As his time in England drew to a close, he saw the wisdom of his choices. Among the few friends he had made were young men from the mosque, two of whom had succumbed to the wiles of western culture. Drink and drugs had befouled their fates and western women, drawn to the novelty of dark flesh, had derailed their resolve to follow Islam. Abdul Massoud had boarded the plane home without even bidding them farewell.

He finished cleaning the scimitar. Holding it aloft, he checked the reflection of sunlight on the blade, ran a thumb down the sharp edge and then gazed with warm satisfaction over his collection of abandoned American military toys.

He had plans for them.

Upon returning to Afghanistan, he had rejoined the Taliban. Stronger than ever in his faith, he had labored patiently through the various stations of his rise to prominence. Even as a young man, he had been marked out for his industry and piety. He loved Allah and Islam with a fervor unmatched by few. He had assumed all his Taliban brothers shared his zeal. And that had proven to be his undoing.

Massoud's favorite passage from the Q'uran:

The oppressed cry out: "Our Lord, take us out of
this city of oppressive people and appoint for
us from Yourself a protector..."

When the Americans came, he had at first felt like his
hour of destiny had arrived. Here at last was a chance for him
to prove his fervor in battle by taking the fight to the infidel
in person. But he had found himself stymied again and again
by senior commanders, whose caution and zeal to protect the
status quo at the expense of making further gains hobbled his
proposals. He had found himself in conflict with a regional
governor. The governor had taken steps to ensure Massoud's
career plateaued where it was. Where he had once been rising
like a rocket among the ranks of the faithful, he was now suddenly persona non grata.

And so he had gone his own way.

By dint of his guts, his brilliance and his absolute ruthless-
ness, he had taken over this section of the country, uniting
bandits and warlords beneath his banner. By creating The Way,
he had cemented control over the minds of his followers and
amassed this fabulous storehouse of infidel weapons.

With a wave of his hand, he beckoned his subaltern Gul
toward him from where he squatted with his cellphone in the
shadow of a Humvee.

"Have the preparations been made?" he asked.

"Indeed they have, O Great One." Gul bowed. "I have spoken
this day with representatives of Crimson Jihad, the Palestinian
Jihad, ISIS and al-Qaeda. All of them have agreed to your pro-

posal. Their representatives hasten here even as we speak."

Massoud smiled in satisfaction and waved Gul away.

And so it begins, he thought.

Shortly, representatives of the major Islamic terror organizations would converge on this base bearing briefcases of cash. Upon their arrival, Massoud would auction off a portion of these munitions. The sales would generate untold millions that he would plough back into his organization. If he could not rise among the Taliban, then he would rise upon a larger stage – that of global terrorism. He would aggrieve the infidel. He would defend the faithful. And he would cleanse the world in blood.

CHAPTER 14

"Sir?" Bob Corbett entered the Oval Office, closing the door to his office behind him. "General Daniels is here with the drone pictures. And we have some further updates on the intel side."

"Yeah. Bring him in." President Harwood dismissed his secretary with a nod and put aside the budget figures he had been reviewing. It was an uncharacteristically slow morning in the West Wing and Harwood was grateful for the opportunity to catch up on paperwork. Now was the perfect time to reveal details of Operation REDEMPTION.

General Daniels entered, came to attention and saluted. President Harwood smiled and stood. "At ease, General. Has Bob briefed you on developments?"

"No, sir. I just got here." Daniels favored Bob Corbett with a nod as he joined them.

"We're going to get your guys." Harwood gestured toward the sitting area by the fireplace, and they took seats. "CIA are tip of the spear in this case. We have an operation currently underway in-country. We're re-tasking those resources with a priority on locating those servicemen."

"Yes, sir. Thank you, Mr. President." General Daniels held up the file folder. "Sir, if I may?"

"Go ahead."

Daniels opened the folder and began laying photographs out on the coffee table. "The base is a large one. The second biggest in the country, in fact. The French essentially seized and refurbished an Afghan Air Force installation that was left over from pre-Taliban days. It's big enough to function as a storage depot for a great deal of equipment. And that's what they've got here." He drew the tip of his finger down one side of a photo. "Here? Tanks. Acres of them. A mixed bag, too. Some of ours. Some Brit tanks. They've also seized jets and helicopters. And apparently enough Afghan pilots have defected to the Taliban side to make those worthwhile acquisitions."

"That's one hell of a lot of hardware," said Harwood, shaking his head.

"We may be able to get more detail on just what's there," said Corbett. "Mr. President, I just finished meeting with the French Deputy Ambassador and his senior intelligence liaison. They're under orders from the French President to furnish us with anything helpful and they're being very forthcoming. The liaison let drop that they have eyes on the ground, in country and not far from the base."

"Afghan locals?"

"Apparently, sir." Corbett shrugged. "The Taliban may be running the government. But the hearts and minds of the people are with us, sir. French intelligence is in contact and tasking them with forward reconnaissance."

"That's Abdul Massoud's neck of the woods," said General Daniels. "Anyone willing to get close enough to gather intel on him has guts to burn."

"Remarkable bravery," agreed the President. "Whoever it is, I want to meet them and shake their hand when all is said and done."

* * * * *

At that very moment, Shakira Nazari was watching a guard with an AK approach the compound where the Americans were being kept. It was the hour before dawn and the desert around the base was still. As she had every morning for the past few days, she had run this way and spent a few minutes observing the base at the urging of Mafuz.

"Tell me as much as you can about the Americans," he had said. "How many are there? How healthy are they? How closely are they being guarded?"

So far she had reported their reduction in number from five to three. Because she was confining her observations to the pre-dawn hours, she had no idea how often the guards came to visit, but it did not seem that regularly. So this morning's lengthy interaction was unusual.

The guard approached the gate, unlocked it and pushed it open. Then he motioned with the AK in a gesture that was unmistakable: *get up and get moving*. Wearily, the three figures rose. Under his watchful eye, they marched out of the compound and through the open gate of the shunt yard into the desert itself. Shakira noted a second man waiting a short distance from the edge of the base fence. He, too, held an AK. Stuck point-down in the sand beside him were three shovels and a shape bundled in a black tarp. As the Americans drew near, he gestured with his AK. The three prisoners each grabbed a shovel and began to dig.

It's a grave, Shakira realized with a shiver. *And the thing in the tarpaulin must be a body.*

When she saw the guards draw off a short distance and light cigarettes, she made a quick decision.

Moving carefully, she edged down from the ridge. There was a pile of boulders perhaps one hundred yards from where the Americans dug. Shakira was cautious to remain behind cover, saving her boldest moves for those moments when the guards' backs were turned. But she was young and lithe and soon able to press up against the boulders. She squinted at the Americans. There were two men and one woman. From the way she carried herself and the men responded, she seemed to be in charge of their little group. Shakira noted the woman had black skin, like her friend Washington who had told her about Jesse Owens. She found this strangely reassuring.

Shakira waited until the guards' backs were turned and the American woman was looking in her direction. Then she stepped out from behind the boulders and waved.

The American woman straightened.

Shakira gave her a thumbs up, like Washington used to do.

The American women grinned and responded with a thumbs up of her own. Then she went back to digging.

Shakira slipped back behind the boulders, then bent her steps for home.

CHAPTER 15

"Echo-Six was a Marine Corps helicopter evac flight out of a forward firebase near Kandahar," said Sara. Ranged before her at the conference table: Cody, Yurgi and David Kent, who acted as translator for the two Afghan tribal commanders also in attendance. "The flight commander was one Lieutenant Kendra Watson, relatively new to piloting and command. Her second in command was named Lieutenant Stefanie Wendell. They lifted off from Kabul Airport and flew the hour inland to the firebase. There they took aboard two Marines and one Army Corpsman. On the way back to KBL, they were shot down. Army intel says there's evidence of surface-to-air missile activity."

At this, the two Afghan commanders murmured together and chuckled.

"I guess they're reminiscing about the good old days again." David Kent sighed. "Apparently they have CIA to thank for trans-shipping thousands of shoulder-mounted Stinger surface-to-air missile units during the war with the Russians…"

One of the commanders said something that caused the other to laugh heartily.

"He said that a few hundred continue to float around the country like, well, the Afghan equivalent of party favors. One turning up is a good sign. Like receiving the orange at a wedding." Kent paused, pondering this for a moment. Then: "I have no idea what that means, sir, but I think its connotation is generally positive."

"Watson's service record is exemplary," Sara continued. "Top marks in all her ratings, enthusiastic and loyal member of the Corps. A born leader. You couldn't ask for a better person to be in charge. There's also Wendell, two Marine riflemen named McKnight and Showalter and an Army medic named Davis."

"Having a medic ups their chances of survival," Cody noted. "Are they all SERE trained?"

"Watson and Wendell are. The two other Marines aren't. Not sure about the medic, but it's unlikely." Sara studied her notes. "The French have an asset on the ground near Massoud's base. That's where Watson and her crew were taken. So there'll be no change in your destination. But the focus of the mission has expanded. Cody's job, in addition to scouting out and confirming the equipment stockpile, is to secure the release of those Marines. You'll receive support from elements in-country. Our source on the ground is located in a village near the base."

One of the Afghani tribal commanders spoke up. Kent translated:

"They know the village. It's one of Massoud's strongholds of support in the region. If there's an intel source there reporting on his activities, they're playing a really dangerous game. Literally putting their lives on the line."

"We'll go in," said Cody. "We'll get those servicemen and women. We'll get hard intel on the base and any equipment there. And we'll take out Massoud in the process."

And when the Afghan tribal commanders smiled at this, Cody knew he had them.

* * * * *

Per arrangement with Yurgi, he and the two Afghan commanders got a 24-hour head start. They would airlift in, connect with local forces and stage up for the trip across the mountains into Panjshir. The delay would afford Cody and Sara the chance to wait on any separate intel that might drop in the meantime. When it came, it was not good.

"The party is down to three. Local source says that two of Marines have died." Although Sara's tone was neutral, Cody could see she was shaken by the news.

"What can you tell me about the source on the ground?" he asked.

"They're controlled be French intelligence, which is gathering and feeding Langley data as fast as they get it. Apparently, the French occupation forces befriended a member of the village and left behind a cellphone."

"Good thinking," he said. "It's certainly paid off."

He was glad he'd have someone local to rely on for intel. Knowing this took a load off his mind as he turned his attention to pulling together his equipment for the mission.

He'd essentially be bushwhacking through mountain country. Langley had obliged by supplying a set of Gore-Tex thermal hiking boots and a versatile military-grade windbreaker with a waterproof wool lining. His Eberlestock X2 pack was loaded with more than sufficient water and rations for the trip, along with a paramedic-grade First Aid kit and GPS uplink. The pack had been modified to store a waterproof computer tablet with onboard Google Earth/GPS cross-linked.

For hardware, he'd use his standard Beretta as sidearm. The rifle he'd been issued was non-standard, but a real treat. The Colt Canadian C8 was a unique weapon – sort of a miniature AR-15 but chambered for standard NATO rounds and able to pack a wallop at close range. The light, compact weapon would hang on a front sling and augment the Beretta. A half-dozen M-67 hand grenades completed his personal armament, leaving him well able to contribute to any combined defense with Afghan forces and well able to care for himself if he became separated from the group.

"I'll remain here with Zinoyev's staff officer," Sara said as they stood together in the doorway of the hangar the night after Yurgi's departure with the local forces. "Comms by radio. Keep us updated, so I can keep Washington in the loop."

"Will do." Cody checked the webbing holding his radio gear in place – throat mike, ear-piece and transmitter.

"And be careful." She smirked. He knew she wanted to kiss

him. He wanted that, too. But this was work. And they had made a deal to put their personal feelings for each other aside whenever they were on the job.

"I'll be careful," he promised.

A cold wind blew across the darkened tarmac. The combat helicopter crew appeared from a side door and approached the chopper that would airlift him into the staging area.

"Go get them and bring them home," she said. "We owe them no less."

CHAPTER 16

Watson waited until the guard secured the padlock and his sandals were crunching away across the asphalt to the shunt-yard gate. She heard it rattle, open and close again. The heavy deadbolt installed after their escape attempt fell into place with a *thunk*. Once that was secure and the sound of the guard's footsteps had receded into the distance, she beckoned for Showalter and McKnight to huddle in close.

"We're not done yet trying to escape. Understand?"

Both men nodded without the slightest hesitation. Davis's death had affected them both, carrying them to sorrowful places that they masked with a warrior's calm silence, but their confidence and morale remained high. Both were hardened ground-pounders, Marines to the core, and up for any action that would frustrate the enemy's plans. Knowing the ranking officer leading their group was also a hard-charger just amped-up their resolve. Watson was pleased with what she saw in these men. The Talis could not have captured a more battle-hardened and dangerous group of Devil Dogs. She vowed then and there to dig deep and do her best by them.

I could be the last commanding officer these men ever have, she reminded herself. *I'll be damned if I let myself be a disappointment.*

"I'm pulling together a new plan," she whispered. "But we've got a sudden break of good luck. Are you ready for this? The locals know we're here. And they're friendlies."

McKnight and Showalter both broke into wide grins and suppressed hoots of glee.

"When they had us out digging that Tali's grave, we were being watched. The guards spent a lot of their time smoking cigarettes with their backs turned. Somebody else noticed, too. It was a girl. Teenager, probably close to eighteen or nineteen. She stepped out from behind some rocks and flashed a thumb's up sign."

"What do you think it means, LT?" asked McKnight. "Think they're planning to come get us?"

"Could be." She shrugged. "But we shouldn't count on that. But here's the thing. This girl didn't have a backpack or vehicle with her. I *did* notice her running shoes, though. She lives close. Which means there's a village nearby."

"I thought we might have passed through one on the way here, LT," offered Showalter. "There was a stretch, a short one, a few miles back. The road smoothed out and things seemed to close in. Through the blindfold, I could hear voices. Some had to be female, no doubt."

"So there's a village close by," said McKnight. "LT, I think we should hump it in that direction."

"That's the plan, guys." Watson grinned, putting her hands to her hips. "The job now is to figure out which way the village lies. That's a problem I want you guys to try and solve while I'm working out the escape plan. Showalter, try and remember everything you can about the trip here. McKnight, see if you can work out compass points and direction from yesterday's grave site. We're going to try and reverse-engineer out little jogger's course."

The men nodded, pleased with the news and pleased to have something to do. Watson applied herself to the task of figuring out the next escape attempt.

* * * * *

There would be no lifting the fence this time. The Talis had set the poles in concrete after the last attempt. Keys were no longer kept in the shunt-yard's vehicles. And the big deadbolt had been put in place at the gate. If anything, their confinement was more impregnable than ever.

If they get tough, we go hard, Watson thought.

It was a strategy that had worked ever since her first jiu-jitsu tournament at age 16. She had fought adult women and learned a thing or two about when and where to press the attack. As often, the best defense had proven to be a good offense. That tournament had seen her pitted against an adult brown belt in the open division. At first, she had thought she was done for. But when the bout began, Watson, a blue belt, channeled her every thought and inhuman focus into the task of beating the older brown belt. The match had proven a battle royal. In the end, she had fought the older woman to a standstill. Her coach had awarded her a purple belt next class.

Go hard ...

Watson resolved that their next attempt would involve a direct assault on the man guarding them. Whether by luring one into the cage or waiting until they were being guided out, they would turn on and overpower the guard holding the AK.

It's usually only one, she thought. *And now we have nothing to lose...*

She watched Showalter and McKnight conferring in a far corner of the cage.

...and everything to gain.

The appearance of the girl was like a beacon of hope. *If* they could overpower a guard, *if* they could get loose, *if* they outpaced their pursuers, *then* they would make for the village.

Watson wasn't naïve. She knew the Talis would follow, and likely subject the village to a massacre if they suspected she and her Marines were hiding there. In fact, she was counting on a posse to be hot on their trail. Her plans depended on their coming close enough to the village to stage an ambush.

We'll hit the team sent to round us up, she thought. *Take their vehicles and weapons and press on.*

She knew the Uzbekistan border was somewhere in this part of the country. Once they were oriented to the compass, they could lay in a course and make for it at top speed. The Uzbeks would likely be suspicious but at least receptive to a group of escaped American POWs. Watson wasn't sure she could count on their protection, but figured they'd at least be sympathetic.

It's a long shot, she thought. But it seemed worth the gamble.

CHAPTER 17

From his seat in the rear of the Uzbek army chopper, Cody couldn't identify the moment when they crossed from Uzbek into Afghani airspace. The country, still being in a state of ruin after the 'American War', had no border pickets or air defense to speak of, and the Uzbek aircrew was keeping mum. Only David Kent, in the seat next to him, seemed to be keeping track of their progress.

"We're over Afghanistan now," he said, checking his watch. "Chances are very good the Taliban has no idea you're here or that an aircraft even breached their airspace."

"I thought you said some Afghan pilots had defected to their cause?"

"They have," affirmed Kent. "But Langley and Air Force intel see no indication they've organized anything like an air traffic plan or combat air patrol for their skies, yet. Truth be told, they're likely more focused on just securing their gains on the ground for now."

"Given the havoc wreaked by the last few wars, they have their work cut out for them," Cody admitted.

"Right now, they have to get the warlords onside," said Kent. "Like I said: in Afghanistan, all politics are local. The Taliban have to prove to the local heavies they have what it takes to impose order. They also have to provide the key incentive." Kent rolled his thumb against his forefinger. "We may have been driven out, but Uncle Sam's greenbacks are still king. Besides – religion only goes so far."

Cody laughed.

There was some chatter on the internal channel. Kent acknowledged the pilot with a clipped, brief reply before turning back to Cody.

"We're about five minutes out from the LZ. And that's where I leave you." Kent checked his watch. "Yurgi and the local NHF contingent will meet up with you when we arrive. They'll take you the rest of the way to the base."

"Yurgi's got a direct line to you?"

"Not direct. But close. We coordinate via Zinoyev's commanders, but they're prompt in relaying communications. You'll have access to me but with a slight delay. Sara Durell will be your main contact and will have operational control at our end."

"Okay." Cody checked his gear one last time. He knew Sara and Kent would be side-by-side at the base in Uzbekistan, so if there were operational adjustments to be made at either the individual or company level, that could be handled. For now, he planned to place himself in the hands of the NHF and trust their vast knowledge of the region and players as fundamental to his mission.

The chopper was lowering itself now, the pitch and whine of the engine taking on a different tone as they descended toward the sand. A storm of grit and pebbles rattled the windows in the final moments before they came to rest with a hard bump.

"Welcome to Afghanistan, Mr. Cody." Kent offered a hand. "Good luck."

Cody dropped from the hatch to the sand. The half-moon hung bright in the cloudless sky, sketching the rocks and vegetation in silhouette. Cody crouched below the prop-wash and ran to the shelter of some boulders. The Uzbek chopper idled, the pilot running a few checks in the green glow of his cockpit lights. Cody cast around for signs of the NHF group that was supposed to meet him.

Nothing.

The chopper was the only indication of a human presence in the area. All around them, the vast landscape of the rocky wasteland stretched into the moonlit distance. There were no noises audible besides the whir of the rotors, no men visible besides the chopper crew. When the bird lifted off, Cody would be all alone...

SchWOOOSH!

He threw himself sideways to the sand. He felt, rather than saw, the impact of the air-to-ground missile that narrowly missed the Uzbek forces chopper. *Where the hell had it come from?* Cody lifted his head above the edge of the boulder in time to spot the Apache attack helicopter wheel around and come in for another attack run.

That's one of ours, he thought angrily.

The American markings had been scrubbed off. No Afghani flags on this, but a stencil print of the Arabic lettering identifying the ship as property of the revolutionary government. The pilot was definitely American-trained; he handled the Apache like he was born to it.

The Uzbek pilot, meanwhile, was wasting no time. Hunched forward in his seat, he was lifting off to engage the enemy bird. Cody had noted the rack of missiles on the Uzbek's chopper's undercarriage. Once he got aloft, that Apache would have something to worry about. Cody watched as the chopper slowly climbed, gaining speed as it gained altitude. The pilot adjusted the stick and began swiveling the nose of his craft toward the other helicopter...

SchWOOOSH... BOOM!

The Uzbek chopper erupted in a cloud of gas and flame. Shrapnel hurtled in every direction as the ship, crew and passengers evaporated in the blast. The light from the explosion lit the desert for miles around and, for a flash-bulb instant, Cody was lit in sharp relief.

Overhead, the Apache twisted, adjusting course. Slowly, it began lowering itself...

Cody made for the nearest ridge, hustling double-time. Odds were excellent they had no idea he was here.

A spray of automatic fire sent him diving for cover. Impact geysers erupted around him. *Him?* Were they coming after *him?* They had to be. Why else...?

Then he was up and moving. The Apache spun and activated its spotlight, its beam groping the dark for a target. Cody found a shadowed cleft between two rocks and sheltered there as the light approached, stabbed at and passed over him. Slowly, methodically, the pilot brought the light back and began working the area in a tight search pattern.

That was when Cody heard voices and saw the shapes of men materialize near the wreckage of the Uzbek chopper.

CHAPTER 18

They moved like moths, quick and furtive in the wind blown by the attacking chopper. With their dark desert robes and the draping of shadows, they seemed to flicker in and out of sight as they appeared first here, and then there. Two thoughts occurred to Cody simultaneously:

Who are they?

And...

What are they doing?

The chopper pilot seemed unaware of their arrival. He continued working his search grid, patiently guiding the Apache up one row of the grid before turning and heading down the next. Hunting Cody amongst the rocks and wreckage of the downed Uzbek chopper. A sudden rage shook Cody as he remembered the chopper crew.

Guys with wives and kids, he thought angrily. For them, a short jaunt across the border to drop off a lone agent should have been a milk run. Instead, they'd bought theirs right here in this war-torn, godforsaken hellscape without even a cross to mark their graves. He had no idea who these dark-robed men were or what they wanted. But one thing was sure – Cody would not allow them to meet the same fate.

In for a penny, in for a pound, he thought.

He launched himself from his hidden cleft, heading directly away from the robed men. They saw him and raised a cry. But when it became clear he was not attacking but retreating, they held their fire. Cody skidded to a stop directly behind the searching chopper, raised and sighted the C8. As it banked into a turn, he squeezed the trigger.

Bullets raked the side of the Apache. The pilot twisted the search light desperately. Two of the men in dark robes were unzipping a long nylon bag. Cody went to one knee, threw the Colt to his shoulder and waited until the searchlight found him. And doused it with four quick shots.

An exultant cry went up from the dark-robed men. The Apache answered with a hail of chain-gun fire. Cody dove for cover as a spray of tracer rounds savaged the ground where he'd been. The chopper was hovering in place, now, the pilot trying to bring additional lights on-line. Cody knew if he dropped low enough, he could count on the glow from the cockpit and landing lights to throw some illumination on the ground.

The two robed men, meanwhile, had opened the nylon bag and succeeded in grappling out a large, rectangular object. As Cody watched, one man crouched while the other lifted and placed the item across his shoulders. Then the crouching man straightened and his hand went to the pistol grip below the rectangular chassis.

There it is! Cody thought with a grin. *The orange at the wedding!*

The robed man with the item on his shoulders widened his stance, squinted into a fixed sight and squeezed the trigger of his pistol grip.

The Stinger surface-to-air missile shrieked to life, a shower of fire blasting from the back end of the launch tube as the rocket engaged. It sped across the short distance between the operator and the Apache, detonating with a massive *wallop!* The Apache seemed to hang in the air, stunned for a long moment before it exploded in a storm of flame and shrapnel. The airframe disintegrated in a fiery howl, tilted then plowed nose-first into the ground.

Cody put up the C8 and watched as two of the dark-robed men strode toward him.

"Nice shooting," he commented.

The tallest of the robed men examined Cody, his bright eyes quick and intelligent in his narrow, bearded face. He took note of the grenades, rifle and sidearm, glanced back at the burning wreckage and spoke. His English was excellent.

"I am Muamar Rashid, son of Mohammed, son of Ali. I have the honor of commanding these brave fighters of the National Resistance Front in our battle against the Taliban bandits who have stolen our country. If you are American then, as a free man, I welcome you to our company."

Cody stepped forward and accepted the greeting Rashid offered in the desert fashion, his right arm extended to grip Cody's forearm.

He said the magic word, Cody thought. *Freedom.*

* * * * *

Rashid led his column of a dozen men a few miles into the scrub, moving at a brisk pace. At his instructions, the men set down their gear and built a stealth fire, digging a deep, narrow hole and filling it with dried kindling. The resulting flames burned high and hot but were barely visible at a dozen paces. One of the men set a teapot to boil over the flames and Rashid gestured for Cody to come sit with him.

"Where in America are you from?" Rashid asked. "I have met American men from Texas, New Mex-i-co and New Jersey."

"These days Maryland, mostly," said Cody. "You interoperated with American troops?"

"Not regular troops, no." Rashid shook his head. "But your... *Special* Forces? I believe that is what they are called. Some of them came and joined our group for a period of time."

One of the younger fighters came bearing glasses of tea. He gave one each to Rashid and Cody.

"At first, we thought they would be too soft for our lifestyle." Rashid laughed softly. "But these men – who called themselves 'Rangers' – came to adopt our ways and earned the respect of my fighters. Working together, we killed many Taliban. We were able to help each other."

"God is generous," Cody said.

"Allahu-ackbar. God is great, indeed. I had thought all the Americans were gone."

"US forces have pulled out of the country," Cody affirmed. "But not all left. A man named Abdul Massoud is holding three of my countrymen at an abandoned French base somewhere near here. I've come to rescue them."

Rashid listened to this patiently. When Cody was done, he nodded once.

"Abdul Massoud is a coward and a dog. He hides behind the Scriptures as an excuse to do violence upon the innocent. Such men are fit only to be spit from God's mouth in contempt." He smiled. "That you have been placed in our path is providential. I know this base. We will guide you there and help rescue your men. And we will kill some of Massoud's men. Both are acts of justice and mercy. *Allahu-ackbar.*"

CHAPTER 19

President Harwood and his Chief of Staff Jim Corbett entered the Situation Room. The Chairman of the Joint Chiefs stood as they came in. He was alone at the conference table. The screens around the room were either darkened or fixed on map images of trouble spots around the world.

"Mr. Chairman. Thanks for coming at this late hour." Harwood and Corbett took their seats. Both had come straight from their residences for this meeting and were dressed casually.

"Not at all, Mr. President." The Chairman touched some folders in front of him. "I've got the updates you asked for as well as some background on the sector and the players. We can start wherever you like, sir."

"First off, how's the mission going?"

"As of this moment..." The Chairman checked his watch. "Your man Cody will have crossed over into Afghanistan. Hopefully, CIA's contacts with the NRF will be there to meet him. Delta Force are staged up on the *Ronald Reagan*. And I've had a phone call with my counterpart on the Indian general staff. He was very curious as to the *Reagan's* mission and asked directly about Afghanistan. Then he volunteered some jets. Seems nobody in that neck of the woods cares much for the Taliban."

Harwood and Corbett chuckled.

"The NRF are surprisingly well-equipped for a grassroots insurgency," the Chairman continued. "Turns out rural Afghans aren't that different from rural Americans. They love their land, and they love their guns. So NRF fighters are mostly self-equipped. Lightly but effectively armed. Knowledgeable about the area. The CIA Director tells me that cultivating NRF contacts is a priority for our intelligence station there."

"You mentioned the French having assets on the ground," Corbett said. "Are they NRF? Or some other group?"

"Actually, no." The Chairman's own surprise was evident as he said: "These people are civilians. Apparently, the village near the French base has a blacksmith who became friendly with the French while their forces were in the region."

"Wait. Did you say a *blacksmith?*" The President frowned.

"Yes, sir." The Chairman grinned. "It's awfully primitive in that area of the country. No phones or electrical service. No railroad. Nearest highway is a day's march away. People have to be pretty self-sufficient out there. A man who can work a forge is worth his weight in gold. I gather the French actually made use of his services for small jobs."

"An entrepreneur!" exclaimed Corbett. "Good for him."

"During this man's contact with the French, he apparently

supplied consistently useful information. He was interviewed by French military intelligence who deemed him trustworthy enough to become a source in the region."

"They were paying him?"

"No, sir. Apparently, his price for keeping the French informed was that his village and its inhabitants receive protection. The man is a village elder."

The President nodded. He liked the guy already.

"When the French departed, they left this man a cellphone."

"He's got eyes on the base?"

"No, sir. Apparently, he has a confederate." The Chairman consulted his notes. "Apparently, our eyes on the ground actually belong to a girl. Excuse me, a young woman."

"Is that so?" Harwood nodded, a slow smirk spreading his features. "Well, I can't say I've ever been a huge fan of women's lib, but in this case...I'm all for it."

"A woman?" Corbett's confusion was obvious. "Given the lack of mobility and basic human rights most Afghan women face, I doubt she's much help!"

"On the contrary, Mr. Corbett." The Chairman tapped the topmost file folder. "Apparently she's an athlete. And she had some contact with American forces while in-country. We interviewed an Army corporal named Washington who was stationed in her sector. He knows the girl. Her name is Shakira. She's a pretty active and serious runner."

"So on her morning jog, she's making a pass by that French base? Reporting back what she sees?"

"That seems to be the size of it, Mr. President."

Harwood nodded thoughtfully. "Once this is all said and done, we're going to do something nice for her and that blacksmith. Bravery like that...?" He trailed off, shaking his head. "Okay, Mr. Chairman. Looks like we've got things sewed up on the intelligence and operational end. Now we need to talk contingencies."

"Yes, Mr. President."

He sighed. "Regardless of whether or not Cody succeeds, we need to strike that base."

"Yes, sir." The Chairman opened another folder. "We have a squadron of F-35s onboard the *Ronald Reagan*. Their commanders have already developed an operational plan. I'm told they can be over the base with less than an hour's notice. Per your instructions, sir, they're loaded with the most lethal ordnance short of tactical nukes that we have available. It will be a saturation bombing run, sir. The base is isolated, so we can strike indiscriminately, without concern for collateral damage to civilians."

"Saturation bombing?" asked Corbett.

The Chairman nodded. "The entire base – every building, every vehicle and aircraft, every member of the enemy forces – will be subsumed in a firestorm that will obliterate everything in its path. Nothing will be left."

"Let's hope to God Cody can get our people out."

An aide entered the room, approached the Chairman and handed him a note. The Chairman unfolded and read it, then turned to the President.

"Sir, I regret to inform you that our intelligence source on the ground has confirmed that two of the Americans appear to have died."

"So we're down to three."

"Yes, sir."

The President stood. "Then time is of the essence. Cody is heading in. He works fast. With any luck, this will be over in a few hours. Thank you, gentlemen."

CHAPTER 20

The NRF company moved out, a loose column moving silently through the scrub brush with Rashid in the lead. Cody remained near the end of the line. He was conspicuous as the only westerner, and the only man not wearing desert robes, so did what he could to remain unnoticed. Remaining back here ensured that he would be the last thing any observer would see and that he could slip away undetected if he sensed his presence might endanger the group.

The NRF soldiers were armed and equipped with the most primitive tools. Yet they comported themselves with a professionalism and discipline Cody had only witnessed among the professional military of developed nations. Training would not have been an issue for these men; every one of them was a seasoned combat veteran. Rashid had mentioned learning the art of soldiering as a youth.

"I was thirteen when the Russians rolled into my country," he'd said. "With my father and brothers, I joined our local militia. I killed my first man at age fourteen. Being a soldier is all I have ever known."

The other men reflected this same grim and winnowing background. Afghanistan had been at war, on and off, since the days of Alexander the Terrible (or, 'Great' depending on who you were talking to). Cody saw that reflected in the careful handling of weaponry, in the determined gait of the NRF men. Cody found himself experiencing a swell of real admiration for these grassroots, mountain-savvy peasant warriors, some of whom didn't even own a pair of shoes. In America, people spoke of *going* to war, because that always meant a battlefield in a foreign land. For these men, the battlefield was right in their own backyard.

Like the Viet Cong, the rural warriors of Afghanistan were organized, determined and effective. Modern nations under-estimated them at their peril. *Guys like this will fight like hell,* Cody thought. Because they fought not for some flag or distant political abstraction. They were fighting for the survival of their homes and family. Such men, Cody knew, were powerful allies.

It was because of their disciplined silence that Cody was able to hear the crunch of rock off to the right and higher up the slope of the mountain they now circled.

Something – or some*one* – was watching them.

Cody dropped to the rear of the line. When the soldier ahead of him was twenty feet away, he ducked off the path into the shadows. Pressing himself beneath a low overhang of rock, he held his breath, closed his eyes and listened.

There.

They were good, whoever they were. Lacking radios and night vision equipment, their tail communicated by sound: a snapped twig, a bird call, a rustle of fabric against stone. Any of those sounds could have emerged naturally from either the desert or the column itself. Based on the unbroken pattern of marching feet, Cody was certain Rashid's men were unaware of the intruders' presence.

He slipped out from under the rock overhang and scanned the slope. In the dim moonlight, he could see movement but could not clearly discern individuals. But shadows and shapes were shifting, gathering and coalescing into bodies of men. When Cody was certain there were none on the slope immediately above his position, he began a furtive climb.

These hills were covered by sparse vegetation. *Not much cover,* Cody thought, ducking behind a bush. At this elevation and from this angle, he had a better view.

Perhaps ten men, armed with AKs and arranged in groups of three and four, were descending the hill toward Rashid's column. Cody noted how they wore black and kept to the shadows with the deft, practiced moves of veteran desert fighters. *Taliban?* Cody doubted it. Then he remembered what David Kent had said about bandit groups controlling sectors of the countryside.

I'll bet that's exactly who they are, he thought.

He watched from above as they coordinated their ambush. Their leader seemed to be coordinating things from the rear. Cody spotted him as he stood and signalled with a sort of 'yip' that Cody assumed was an imitation of local wildlife. The sound drew no reaction from the column. And by then, the bandits were descending on them.

With a whoop, the first group of men waded into the column, firing their rifles into the air and screaming threats. Rashid's men rallied, making ready to resist. Then Cody saw the method to the bandit leader's madness. *He's got a line of riflemen with weapons trained on the column,* he realized. The bandit leader stood, his back to Cody, arm raised within view of the riflemen. *Any resistance and they open fire.*

Rashid saw them, too. With a cry, he got his men's attention. Cody did not understand what he said next, but the gesture he made – lowering his hands to the ground, palms first, fingers splayed – was clear. His men were to lower their weapons and offer no resistance.

Like bandits anywhere, the Afghans were more interested in taking goods than lives. The group down below set about disarming Rashid's men, piling their rifles off to the side and shaking down individual soldiers for money, food, ammo. In this country, such a move was tantamount to executing them then and there, for men did not last long out here without those basic necessities.

Rage simmered within Cody. The bandits had already cost them time in their march to Massoud's base. Now they were stripping the NRF of any chance of mounting an attack. The time had come to put an end to this.

The bandit leader was chuckling now. Their objectives reached, he lowered his arm and watched as his riflemen stood and joined their comrades on the path below. Then, with great dignity, he threw back his shoulders, puffed out his chest and began descending the hill to join his men.

He was barely a dozen yards from them when Cody slipped up behind and grabbed the man in a chokehold, pressing the Beretta against his ear.

CHAPTER 21

For a moment, all was stillness.

They stood frozen in tableau: the captured soldiers, the armed bandits and Rashid himself. Then Rashid moved, lightning fast, toward the nearest armed bandit. Seizing his AK, he reversed it, slammed the rifle butt into the bandit's jaw and then leveled the weapon on the rest, barking an order in Pashtu. As one, they dropped their guns.

"Come on," Cody snarled. He released the bandit chief and shoved him forward, the Beretta trained on his head. The man stumbled, turned and shot Cody a hateful glare then resumed walking, head high, his chest still puffed out.

The NRF fighters moved quickly, grabbing up their own fallen weapons and those of the bandits, too. In moments, they had their attackers kneeling in a line, hands on their heads as Cody followed the leader into their midst.

"Tarak Khan." Rashid said the name calmly, without a trace of emotion. Looking to Cody, he added: "The bandit leader here in this region."

"You call *me* a bandit?" Khan snapped in English. "You guerillas are the bandits! Bringing misery to the villagers with your extortions, your demands for weapons and tribute!"

"We extort no one!" Rashid shot back. "We fight for the people!"

Khan stood frozen for a moment at these words. Then he shook his head in disbelief, gazing at the ground and chuckling. "Fight for the people," he said, as though turning the very concept over in his mind for the first time. "You don't even *know* the people! And now you make alliance with…*Americans!*"

He whirled on Cody and spat.

"Barbarians! *Cowards!* The *misery* you have brought to this country! And so many others!" He marched right up to Cody, not stopping until his chest pressed the muzzle of the Beretta. "You ran like *dogs* and left your so-called 'allies' behind. You claim to fight for freedom and liberty? *Whose* freedom? The freedom of the wealthy! Of the big oil companies! Of the military contractors! *That's* the freedom you stand for! The freedom to exploit and enslave! You disgust me!"

And Cody sensed something shift. It was intangible, like an odor or intuition but definitely there. The mood of the group – the kneeling bandits, the soldiers covering them, even Rashid himself – seemed to change. Like water pressed between two panes of glass, it crept forward in an ever widening, spreading arc. Many of the men present who spoke English agreed with some of what Khan said. And they whispered the translation to others.

All alone deep in enemy territory, Cody felt his support from the group ebbing. He had to hand it to Khan. The man knew how to work a room. When he began speaking, Rashid translated for him.

"We came because we were attacked," Cody said. "We stayed because we refused to leave behind a nation in shambles. And we left because we had no choice. I've listened and learned from your tribal commanders, from men like Rashid, about the history here. Empire after empire has come here and failed. I believe that's because the Afghan people value freedom more highly than their own lives. My countrymen who died here laid down their lives for yours."

And Tarak Khan laughed.

"Oh, for *freedom* you laid down your lives? Then those lives were wasted in vain." He flicked a hand vaguely westward. "You know who rules this province? The madman, Abdul Massoud. The 'great imam' and guardian of the Q'uran. The man is dogshit! And this is who is left in charge after your departure? Tell me again about refusing to leave a nation in shambles! Because you Americans have done *worse!* You've left us enslaved!"

Cody almost had them. But Khan had swung the balance of support back toward himself, with gains. He could see it reflected in the faces of the listeners. And he was starting to get a little pissed with the guy.

"But then again!" Khan grinned. "Slavery was *always* America's great institution! You fought a civil war to end it. But, learning you could not survive without it, you didn't. Instead, you just began exporting it abroad!"

Cody worked to control his breathing. The guy was starting to get under his skin and that was not good. Having someone under your skin is when bad decisions get made, missteps. And

Khan knew it. *He's a good tactician, I'll give him that,* Cody thought.

"You hate Abdul Massoud? He's our enemy, too," Cody shot back. "He's got a great store house of weapons –"

"Yes! We know it well! Weapons left behind by you!"

"Yes, abandoned when we left. Now he's gathering it all together for God knows what purpose! And who will pay? Not the military contractors! Or the oil companies! It will be the people whose freedom you claim to care so much about!"

Cody had scored a point. He saw it in Khan's face. The sneer was gone. Something like respect was crowding the edges of his facial expression. The man knew a formidable opponent when he saw one.

"I'm here to take the fight to Massoud." Cody pointed. "Out that way is his base. He's holding some of our people. We're going to go there and get them out. We're destroy his stockpile of weapons. And we're going to kill Massoud if we can."

"Brave words." Tarak Khan was shaking his head again. "And a noble cause, I grant you. Alright, we've come to a stalemate. You let us go, and we'll let you go. But. You cannot pass through my territory. Go back the way you came and circle around."

"Where?" demanded Rashid. "What is the border of your territory?"

"The big *wadi* where the train track meets the foot of the mountains."

"Ridiculous!" Rashid stomped a foot. "You expect us to trek through the mountains to his base? That would take weeks!"

"Then what do you propose to do? Kill us all?" Khan repeated this in Pashtu for his men's benefit. "I promise you that if you kill Tarak Khan and his men, no village in this region will be safe for the NRF. You call me a bandit? The villagers around here call me their benefactor! I have real support from real people! Not from religious nuts in Kabul or greedy oil men in Washington, but mothers and fathers and children! People whose lives I see *everyday!* I do not demand tribute from the villagers! I *give* to the villagers! With my raids on the wealthy and powerful, I have no *need* of their meagre stores! Instead, I work to increase them. For *this* is the *true* Islam! *Zakat!* A giving of alms to ease the sufferings of the poor! I've killed, yes. I've stolen, yes! But may Allah be pleased with my *zakat.* And forgive my sins."

"Allahu-ackbar," said Rashid. And many of the men around echoed him.

Cody realized in that moment that Khan, whatever his faults, lived according to a code that was universally and deeply embedded among the people of this country. He had to grudgingly admit that there was a flake of reason – *honor,* even – in the bandit leader's words and deeds. And those words and deeds had the power to move and influence men, as they were now doing. For in addition to being aware of all these thoughts, Cody was also aware of how the kneeling bandits were side eyeing each other and stabbing furtive glances toward the feet and legs of the distracted NRF men. The tide was turning. Soon they would feel confident enough to make a move. Something, somehow, had to give.

And that's when he made his decision.

"There's another way." Cody holstered the Beretta. "You."

He pointed at Khan. "And me. Here. Now. No weapons. If I win, we can cross your territory. And if you win –"

"Your death will be my prize," spat Khan.

"Okay." Cody smiled. "Let's go."

CHAPTER 22

"You are sure you want to do this?" Rashid's question held a tone of worry.

"It's a quick, flexible solution to a complex problem." Cody unbuckled his utility belt and handed it across, the holstered Beretta a drop-weight dangling at the heavy bend. He unsnapped the sling supporting the C8 and handed it to the man Rashid ordered forward. Cody gave him the grenades and the rest of his kit, as well.

Now the two sides, the NRF and Khan's bandits, had formed up facing each other across the sand. The bandits were still behaving themselves as the NRF still had their weapons, but they held themselves with renewed pride and confidence. Their leader was about to redeem their honor.

Or so he thinks. Cody measured his opponent.

Khan was a big man, broad-shouldered with fists the size of ham hocks. *Those would sting,* he thought. It was impossible to tell under the robes what shape the man's lower body was in but there was no particular reason to believe it would be any less muscled than the top half. Cody was about to face a monster. There was no doubt Khan would know how to handle himself physically. The question was the extent of his training.

I'm about to find that out, he thought.

Khan glared across the space between them, his fists opening and closing as he breathed loudly and heavily. Like a bull working itself up to charge. Which was exactly what he did the moment Cody turned around. Cody moved out to meet him, veering left at the last instant and sending the big man charging into his ranks of followers. Cody turned and watched as the group of unarmed bandits grasped and propelled their chief back into the arena with shouts of encouragement.

He and Cody were circling now, fists up, drawing ever close toward one another. Khan swung. Cody ducked and the punch missed. Then he came up from under and slammed the heel of his right palm into the left side of Khan's chest as hard as he could. The open-palm technique was brutal, designed to send a shockwave inward toward the heart. Depending on the health of the target, the blow can sometimes kill. Its impact was variable, but the technique held one constant: it was never pleasant.

The blow landed. Khan gasped. Cody saw his eyes widen in shock before he flailed his arms and backed away. The rhythm of his breathing was broken. And he was keeping a slightly wider distance now.

Bullseye!

Cody went in again, He feinted with a low kick, then went in with a backfist that connected with Khan's jaw. *That's two!* One of the men in the NRF snickered. The laughter stung

Khan into motion. He bellowed and charged.

Cody dodged to the side, but the move was anticipated. With canny prescience, Khan barreled in, switching direction at the last moment to catch and tackle him. Cody went down, all two hundred pounds of the massive desert bandit crashing atop of and winding him.

"American pig! Coward! Dog!"

Khan struggled to get the mount, to start throwing punches from on high. But Cody had three months of jiu-jitsu from Fort Bragg and swept him from mount with a quick move. Khan hit the sand, then Cody hit Khan. In the face over and over.

Then he was up, fists raised, circling again.

Khan rolled to all fours, panting. A mixture of blood and drool dangled from his lips. His breathing was a labored wreck. Trembling, he stood. Threw back his head. And came forward with his fists raised.

Cody went in to strike –

...and got a face full of sand.

Khan had grasped and held a handful of pebbly soil on his way back up from the deck. The simple ploy was enough to surprise Cody, forestall any attack and leave him vulnerable in the time it took to wipe his face. And Khan exploited that.

Cody brought his arms up reflexively, palms to ears, elbows forward, caging his head. So when Khan's haymakers fell on him, they hit wrist and knuckle, not eyes and nose, The bandit chieftain roared and seized Cody by the back of the head, driving his face downward toward a knee strike. But Cody's elbows trapped the blow, deflected it. Then he was straightening and backing away and men from both sides were muttering their surprise.

"Tarak Khan is tiring..."

"The American looks strong!"

"...going to be blood..."

Cody kept his boxing stance, his weight on his back foot, on the defensive for now. Tarak Khan was circling, his arms raised high, his breathing heavy. He came in again, howling, his arms pinwheeling back and forth, throwing the folds of his robe wide as a distraction.

Cody dodged aside, grabbed a fold of robe and swept Khan's nearest ankle. The bandit leader went down with a crash. Still, Cody hung back, giving his opponent time to rise. He had to be seen as giving Khan a fair chance, or else his victory would be seen as dishonorable and therefore meaningless. This wasn't personal – not for Cody, anyway. This was about earning the right to pass through the man's territory, nothing more. Violating the rules of fair play might be taken as license to violate the terms of the duel. He had to move carefully.

And he had to humiliate Khan.

There was no other way for it to go down.

The bandit leader had risen again. Cody noted the open palms, the lack of any handfuls of sand. He also noted the strained expression on Khan's face, the beard soaked in perspiration and spittle, the labored breathing. But there was still a fierce light in the man's eyes. And when he lowered his head and charged, it was with everything he had left. Cody had to respect the man. Tarak Khan might be many things, but a coward was not one of them.

He and Cody collided in the center of the clearing. A flurry of punches rose and dropped. Two of Khan's landed, stunning Cody and driving him back. The bandit leader pressed forward, his men shouting encouragement. That's when Cody drew back two full paces, crouched and delivered a spinning back kick to the onrushing Khan. The boot heel connected with the exact center of Khan's solar plexus, and the bandit leader went down.

Cody withdrew and stood in a crouch, his fists raised, ready. Khan did not move.

"Enough." Rashid stepped in, waving his arms. "Enough. Your leader fought well but he's defeated."

Below him, Khan made a groaning sound and rolled to all fours. He spat and wobbled to his feet, clearly stunned. But he waved off all offers of help.

"It is done," he said. "You've won, American. You and your men may pass. I was wrong to call you cowards. I say this in the presence of Allah and my men. You fought well."

Cody nodded. "You, too. And we promise – we won't cause any trouble in your territory." He smiled. "Not for you, anyway."

Tarak Khan wiped the blood from his lips, looked Cody in the eye and laughed. "For that," he said, "I am glad."

* * * * *

They resumed their trek in darkness. After a time, Rashid fell into step beside Cody.

"You were wise not to main or kill Tarak Khan," he said quietly. "Wiser still not to humiliate him utterly. Although a bandit, Khan observes the *Pashtunwali,* the warrior code. No man can deny him this honor."

"And what is that code?"

"The three pillars are honor, hospitality and revenge."

Cody smirked. "So I can expect revenge?"

"No. Because you showed honor, you shall receive hospitality."

CHAPTER 23

Damn if I haven't figured it out, Watson thought.

She knew it would come. Sooner or later, it would tumble, like the bolt of a lock or the lucky dice landing with just the perfect split. She had worked for a time at Walmart and become friends with the store detective, a crusty old ex-highway patrol officer with a flair for busting shoplifters.

"I can make a thousand mistakes," he used to say. *"All they have to make is one. That's enough for me to catch them."*

And sure enough, the Tali guard had made his mistake. That is to say, he had fallen into a pattern where guarding the Marine prisoners was concerned. He would have been urged by his superiors to avoid the trap of repetition, of repetition becoming routine, of routine becoming habit. And, for the most part, he had done so. Except for this one thing.

Every day he opens the shunt yard gate. He crosses the yard. Twenty-two steps. Then he pulls out keys and unlocks the lock. There is a pause as he puts the lock in his belt pouch. Then he slides the chain free.

The pause during which he stowed the lock. *That* was the deadly habit. The one Watson intended to exploit.

She began priming McKnight and Showalter. Without telling them why just yet, she nevertheless had them practice listening for the shunt-yard gate. The moment it opened, they sprinted to the gate of their enclosure and took up runner's "on your marks" position. Per Watson's instructions, they held these until the chain rattled as it was pulled out. In the seconds before the gate opened, they would relax to a normal stance.

"So what's the play, LT?" Showalter asked at their next staff meeting. "Are you gonna tell us why we're getting ready on the sprinter's marks like that?"

"Because we're going to rush the gate," Watson explained. "I've got our guard's routine down. I know how he rolls, and he's lazy. Leaves the gate to the shunt-yard open, even. If we jump that dope and haul ass we can get through to the airfield and the line of choppers beyond."

"Can you fly us out, LT?"

"Oh, yeah." Watson flexed her fingers open and closed. "Just let me get my hands on the stick of one of those Apaches and I'll fly us home. And on the way out, I'll rain more fire and hell down on this place than God ever laid on Sodom and Gomorrah."

CHAPTER 24

Jack Cody had spent a lengthy career in covert operations. He had attended every course in professional development, from seminars on intelligence sourcing at the Pentagon special war college to advanced bushcraft sponsored by the US Ranger Command. He was generally accepted to be one of America's top five special forces operators for navigating foreign territory, sight unseen. But he learned more from Rashid and his men in three hours marching time than all those professional development hours combined.

He began to understand why Afghanistan was such a hard nut to crack. Having served alongside Middle- and Near Eastern soldiers before, he knew them to be solid operators. But something about their patterns of movement – their rhythm and cadence – had always puzzled him. He had consulted on the matter with senior officers and voiced harsh opposition to any who suggested it was the result of laziness or ineptitude. Now he got it.

The sand and shadows shift, he noted. *And they shift with them.*

It was amazing – hypnotic, even – to watch these black-clad sand ninjas slip in and out of the shadow and from behind the cover of every bush, rock and wall that presented itself. It was almost like ballet, the way these guys moved together. When they reached the outskirts of the village near the base and the voices of dogs rose, sounding the alert, he began to despair.

The last time he'd worked with the IDF, they had moved into an area of the Gaza controlled by Crimson Jihad. Scouts had gone ahead of the main body to survey the perimeter of the villages. Their Uzis, Cody's guide had explained, were equipped with silencers in case they encountered dogs. Many rural Palestinians kept their mutts chained in the yard at night to guard the chickens and such. They barked whenever IDF appeared, as well. The payment for their vigilance was often a bullet.

Not so among Rashid's men. As they came to a village near their final destination, three young scouts had taken off to muffled laughter, each bearing a bag of some moist, heavy substance. They'd returned shortly, the dogs' voices silenced.

"Nice, juicy rib bone," Rashid chuckled. "We don't shoot those animals. We buy them off. Like we buy off Taliban." And he laughed again, louder this time.

Their journey continued, skirting that village and then traversing a wide valley. At last ,they came to the outskirts of Rashid's home. "Welcome!" He clasped Cody's shoulder. "It's my honor to introduce you to my family. Come."

Cody watched as the core of Rashid's men peeled off, each in his own separate direction, to a dwelling of his choosing. *This must be home base,* Cody thought. This would be Rashid's home village, the center of his power. *Because the only politics that matters in Afghanistan is local,* Cody thought, remembering David Kent.

Rashid brought them down a narrow side street – more of a goat path than an alley. One branch of the path curved up to a low wooden doorway upon which he rapped twice. It opened promptly.

The wizened face that appeared from within was the smooth, hairless oval of an elderly woman. Of course, all women in Afghanistan wore at least the hijab with their hair covered. But this one's seniority was obvious from the look on her face, from her tone of voice and her thunderous frown.

"This is my grandmother," said Rashid respectfully. He turned and spoke to her in their native tongue for a long minute, which stretched to two. The older woman snapped a few sharp words, stabbing her eyes Cody's way when she did. At length, she clammed up, arms crossed, glaring at him with suspicion for a few seconds before muttering a few words at Rashid.

"She says you are American. Wants to know why you've come."

"I've come to rescue my friends," he told her.

And, upon hearing this, the aged Afghan widow pulled open her door and stood aside, welcoming them in with the blessings of their home.

* * * * *

With the simple hospitality of the desert, she welcomed them. And made Cody feel like a king.

"The westerners have come our way for centuries," Rashid

translated as she spoke, bending to fetch her kettle and run fresh water into it from an Aquatainer's spigot. "We have learned to question them when they come. If they offer abstract answers – strange and convoluted responses – we disregard them as insincere. You speak of friends. The captured Americans at the base."

"Yes." Cody and Rashid shared a look of surprise. "You...?"

But then she was turning, raising a hand to cup her mouth and calling: "Shakira! Shakira, girl!"

Rashid smiled. "She is calling out to my niece. Shakira lives here with her grandmother. She knows the area around here very well."

Cody heard the thump of footsteps. Around the edge of a doorway, a girl's face appeared, and she lit up when she saw Rashid. She began speaking to him in their language before seeing Cody, at which point she switched to English.

"Here is my Uncle Rashid, the brave guerilla leader," she teased. "I wonder. Did he remember to bring his beloved niece a present?"

Rashid laughed. "You always claim I promised to bring you presents when I never did!"

"See how he changes his story?" Shakira came in, shaking her head in mock lament, linking her arm through Rashid's. "The poor devil makes boastful promises of generosity when he leaves that he fails to live up to upon arrival. We indulge him in this eccentric behavior. Because it allows him, however briefly, to feel like a wise and generous man!"

And Rashid was bent double with laughter now. The special bond between uncle and niece was evident. Shakira was obviously a remarkable girl, Cody thought. This belief was only confirmed when she turned to him and asked:

"Have you come to rescue the Americans at the base?"

CHAPTER 25

Later that afternoon, Cody ducked into the back room Rashid's
grandmother had indicated was for his use. He fished his sat
phone from his backpack, powered it up and engaged the secure, encrypted line to Sara. By now she and the Uzbek liai-
sons would have moved to the forward operating area by the
Afghan border to monitor his progress. She answered on the
second ring.

"Been wondering when we'd hear from you."

"It was quite a hike to get in here. No sign of Yurgi. Our
chopper was blown away by one of Massoud's pickets. I've tak-
en up with a different NRF cell. A man named Rashid."

He gave her time to key that into her computer for analysis.

"They've brought me to the village we're getting intel from."

"That checks out." He heard relief in her voice. "That sector
of the Panjshir Valley is where the cell signal is coming from.
The French gave us the coordinates as part of our intel pull.
Your man Rashid has a good reputation with both our people

and the French. Tribal commander. A Tajik and very anti-Taliban. The government in Kabul has a million-dollar bounty on his head. You're in good company."

"Roger that. And we've got an unexpected bonus. One of the locals, a girl, makes daily passes by the base on her morning runs."

"*Morning runs?*" He could hear incredulity straining her voice. "Cody, are you sure? Women in that part of the country can't even step foot out of the house unless they're wearing a *burqa*. You've seen those things. You're telling me this Afghan teenager goes for a run wearing one? That's impossible. They're like hazmat suits."

"No. She just wears field gear. A shirt, some pants, a cap to hide her face. I'm going to accompany her tomorrow morning. Do an onsite reconnaissance of the base. See if I can spot our prisoners."

"An extra before-action recon is a benefit. Go for it. Meanwhile..." During the pause, he heard her clicking computer keys. "We have some intel we've pieced together cross-referencing info from our runner... I'm thinking we should give her a code name? Anyway, we cross referenced intel from her and some images we downloaded from the Keyhole satellite. You recall she mentioned seeing a convoy of vehicles headed for the base?"

"Yeah."

"We've spotted another one. Near as we can tell, they're terrorist cronies of our guy, Massoud."

"Sounds like he's planning a little fire sale." Cody shook his head. "It's the obvious move. Sell off some of his stockpile to finance his enterprise. Use the rest to wage war."

"On who?"

"The Taliban, probably. My guess is he'll start a guerilla campaign, taking one province at a time. A leaner, more virulent version of fundamentalist Islam. He'll sweep away the old and supplant it with the new." Cody looked up at the ceiling. "It will be the price they pay for having ignored him."

* * * * *

And oh, yes. Shakira could run.

Cody could power through just about any distance on a run. But his technique was essentially military-style, designed to hump it over long distances quickly. His movements bore no resemblance to the fluid, distance-demolishing strides of the girl. She was a natural, moving more like a gazelle than a human being. And she had obviously done some reading or gotten some coaching, because her technique was refined.

Raw talent and a lot of hard work, Cody thought, regulating his breathing to keep pace with her. *That's a winning combination.*

Shakira guided them along the rough desert roads until they reached a low rise. He followed as she began scrambling up toward the ridge. At one point, she paused, one hand on a rock to steady herself, and turned back.

"The base is a quarter-mile down behind this ridge," she said. "They don't always have guards this far out, but sometimes. Be on your guard, okay?"

"Sure." Cody smiled. "I appreciate the heads-up."

She was a remarkable kid. No doubt about it. Regardless of her talents as a runner, a future as a wife and mother was what lay in store for Shakira. Cody found himself wondering what sort of a man she would choose for a husband. A remarkable young woman like her – stubborn, determined, disciplined – would have a high bar set for any potential partner. Cody couldn't imagine the sort of man capable of reaching it.

They ran along just below the summit of the ridge for half-an-hour. Then Shakira stopped, gazed up at the top and crouched low. Cody followed her lead, creeping along behind her until he could step to one side and peer over the ridge next to her.

Beyond lay the base. It took up the entire length and breadth of the wide valley it occupied. *They weren't kidding when they said he had a stockpile of equipment,* Cody marveled. There was row on row of tanks, some of them cutting edge technology. He saw other tanks, older models, along with APCs, G-wagons, flatbed trucks, artillery and rows of helicopters. It was one of the largest concentrations of fire power Cody had ever seen in a single place.

"Come." Shakira touched his elbow. "I'll show you where your countrymen are."

She led them along the ridge several hundred yards to a quiet corner of the base. Cody recognized the type of vehicles mustered there. *Maintenance trucks, repair vehicles,* he thought. It was a glorified shunt-yard.

"Look."

There in the far corner, partially concealed by an enclosure swaddled in translucent plastic, were three figures wearing the worn fatigues of United States Marines.

"That's them, alright," said Cody. "No doubt about it."

"You'll rescue them?"

"If it's the last thing I do."

CHAPTER 26

Again, the quiet column moved through the desert night. Rashid led the way.

Cody's job was to identify and confirm the location of abandoned American weapons. But he planned to do more than just surveillance. With Rashid's help, he had sourced ten pounds of C-4 explosive and remote detonators. He planned to stop and wire up as much equipment as possible while making his way across the base. Detonating it once he had located and sprung the POWs would create the perfect diversion and set Massoud's men on edge, impairing their efficiency. Rashid had grinned when Cody told him that part of the plan.

"We will slaughter them like dogs," he'd promised, then gone to tell his men.

The desert was quiet. An eerie wind shook the unearthly stillness, rising like a voice in the dark to moan briefly and then subside. The column of NRF fighters made barely a sound: the burlap wrapping in which they swaddled their feet muffled their steps and left no tracks. Again, Cody was impressed. Most of these guys looked pretty wild and hairy. None would pass a boot camp inspection. But once they pulled it all into one sock and went operational, they were as good as any commando squad Cody had ever seen. Almost – though not quite – at special forces tier.

Now the base fence line was ahead. The column stopped and, as one, the men knelt in a crouched position. Clipped whispers in the night: Cody's name – a motioning forward. Moving in a low duck-walk, he made his way up to Rashid's position and slipped in beside him.

"Praise Allah, praise His infinite mercy and goodness. We are blessed as the inheritors of His sacred word," Rashid was whispering. Turning to Cody, he said: "If a warrior places his trust in God and engages the enemy, he cannot go far wrong."

The plain faith in those words, and the simple sincerity of Rashid's piety, moved him. He was not a man to speak of God, but he answered: "I believe that's true."

"Do the warriors of your land pray before battle, friend Cody?"

"Many do. Yes."

"Most are Christian?" Rashid seemed genuinely curious.

"Many different faiths are represented in our armed forces." He thought for a moment. "In the special forces community, there are many men who are Christian. But Native Americans are also well represented. I don't know who they pray to."

"Allah hears all our prayers." Rashid sounded confident. "He has led you here to rescue your friends. God is great. But we will not rely on faith alone. My men will position themselves for attack and wait for your signal. What will that be?"

"The first explosion," he said. "I'll wire up as much of the equipment as I can on the way in. Once we're ready to exfil, I will start a sequence of detonations. If you time your attack to coincide with them, the enemy will be convinced it's a major attack. We'll slip out and rendezvous with you here."

"Go with God."

Cody nodded and moved out.

* * * * *

He crept forward, imitating the tactics he had observed from the NRF fighters. There was little ground cover between Rashid's position and the base, but Cody made the most of what was there: a few large thorn bushes, a dry riverbed, ample piles of loose rock. He made it to the edge of the fence line and crouched next to a heap of boulders just over three feet in height. Hunkering down into their shadows, he thought through next steps.

The air-strike would go forward, regardless of whether or not he reported back a bullseye on the munitions stockpile. Only a negative from him would stop it. Silence would be concluded to mean catastrophic mission failure due to injury or death, which was confirmation enough. Jets would rocket from the deck of whatever carrier was nearest and visit the high-kiloton wrath of the United States upon any living organism on that base. But that firepower would be more accurately directed, and the deployment made that much more effective with the aid of Cody's recon. So he made ready.

Loaded into the Eberlestock X2 pack, in addition to the plastique and detonators, was a SiOnyx Aurora IR Night Vision camera. Each top-of-the-line digital image capture could be downloaded to Cody's sat-phone for instantaneous, real-time intel sharing with Sara back at the base on the Uzbek border. She would relay the images back to the carrier for use by mission planners.

And by then, me and those American POWs will be long gone, he thought. Given the ordnance likely to be chosen for the strike, they would likely feel the ground shake even back in the village.

He crept forward, keeping low to the scrub. illumined in silhouette from the base arc lights were the outlines of tanks. Cody could glimpse no sentry. And he knew that cultural prohibitions made the use of dogs by observant Muslims unlikely. So unless the fence was wired, he was confident he faced little in the way of early warning systems.

Reaching the fence, he removed his phone from his pocket. The cord he produced plugged into a data port at one end. The other terminated in a set of steel clamps. He opened a CIA app called CrossWindz3 and attached the clamps to the fence. Receiving no signal, he breathed a sigh of relief. The fence was neither electrified nor alarmed. He could climb or cut through at will.

A multi-tool in an exterior pocket of the Eberlestock included a set of military-grade wire clippers. Kneeling by a pole,

Cody snipped out a triangular section of fence, pushed it down and crawled through. Once inside, he produced four black zap-straps and secured the fence back in place. Then he rose.

He heard the hum of a distant generator, flips and flutter of pennants attached to vehicle aerials snapping in the moaning wind that rose occasionally in the night.

It was time to get going.

CHAPTER 27

From his current position, the Americans were in a stock-ade-like structure a quarter of a mile away, due south. Cody sprinted in a low crouch across the lit distance separating him from the first row of tanks. He flashed across, being in the light for barely five seconds. But as anyone who has ever done special ops knows, five seconds is not the flicker civilians see but rather a small eternity. Five seconds was more than ample time for even the laziest watch tower detail to catch a glimpse of him. But as he crouched in the shelter of the nearest tank, he counted, waiting. Ten. Twenty. Fifty. One hundred. No hue and cry.

Nothing. He rose from his haunches and examined the nearest tank. The low chassis, elongated main gun and squat turret was of no American design. A quick once-over told him everything he needed to know.

This one's an old Soviet T-54, he thought with wonder. No telling how old it was. That Massoud had rounded up Russian as well as American hardware for his little auction suggested he was approaching it as a fire sale. Still – whether Russian or American, this tank seemed as good a place as any to start.

Working quickly, he searched through his pack for the first square of C-4. Wrapped in wax paper, it had the feel and heft of a quarter stick of butter. Cody removed it, unwrapped the paper and crouched beside the T-54. Reaching up under the tread well, he pressed the gooey plastique to the underside of the tank chassis. Then he produced a remote detonator that was about the same size as a roll of Lifesavers. He pushed on one end, activating the blinking red light of the receiver he would trigger from his phone. Then, leaning in, he pressed the detonator into the plastique and got moving.

The noses of the tanks stretched ahead into the light. But the space behind them was shadowed, and so Cody sprinted along past a series of T-54 tail fins. He guessed he passed about twenty when the tank profile changed to armored car.

Panhards, Cody recognized. Massoud's base was turning out to be a veritable museum. *He's rounded up every damn bit of hardware he can get his hands on.* It must have required a staggering level of planning and coordination. These French armored tanks were 1970 models at best. But like so much left in the arid Afghan sun, they had been well preserved and obviously kept in good repair. Cody imagined that some of the most widely experienced military mechanics in the world must live in the region. *Who else could keep all this in top repair?*

After the Panhards came a row of Abrams and Cody stopped again. This time he climbed up top and pressed two sticks of plastique to the underside of one's turret, ensuring the resulting detonation would blow the gun emplacement sky-high. He would make sure these blasts would provide a memorable fireworks exhibition.

In the spirit of 1776. And all in good fun. Of course.

He came to the end of that row of vehicles and saw, one hundred yards distant, a line of choppers. His heart jumped in recognition of the familiar silhouette and design. *Apaches!* Row upon row of America's latest high-tech helicopter gunships lined the field, stretching as far as the eye could see.

And somewhere close by? The enclosure containing the Marines.

Cody advanced into the shadows, keeping low. He crossed the dark land bridge between the tanks and choppers. Reaching the nearest one, he decided to do a daisy-chain: four in a row. Over the course of the next twelve minutes, Cody wired up four Apaches, alternating wired and unwired choppers to maximize the impact of the explosions. He was just completing the fourth when he identified the direction of the generator.

He heard the humming. It was close. Closing his eyes helped him get a better fix...

There.

Swiveling his head in that direction, he opened his eyes. And sure enough, tucked among the taller bodies of helicopters was the roof of a low tin structure. There was a light by the open front wall. And not a soul in sight.

Cody finished the fourth chopper and made for the generator poste-haste. The Marine enclosure was visible from here. Cody kept flashing glances toward it as he stashed a hidden block of C-4 below the generator. At a dead run, he could be there in just over a minute. He finished positioning the explosive, armed and inserted the detonator. And was halfway to the enclosure when a noise intruded from above. He looked up.

One of the Huey gunships was making an approach. Craning to see, Cody noted a small heliport had been cleared in the middle of the base. The set-up had the look of everything you'd need to stage out of here – an air traffic hut, a headquarters, a row of pre-fab Quonset huts at the distant edge of the landing/parade ground. With a last glance at the Marine enclosure, Cody crept to the edge of the landing zone.

The Huey landed and began powering down. The hatch slid open to reveal a half-dozen men in military fatigues emerged, crossing the floodlit landing area to one of the Quonset huts. As the door opened, Cody heard a hubbub of voices, a radio. *That would be enlisted quarters,* he thought.

The pilot, meanwhile, took his time. Cody watched as he finished a clipboard of paperwork in the green light of the cockpit, then switched the light off and made his way aft. He appeared at the hatch before jumping down and crossing to the ops building. By Cody's reckoning he was inside barely five minutes – just long enough to make his report. He would be tired after the day's work – tired and eager to grab some rack time.

And sure enough his suspicions were confirmed. The pilot emerged a few minutes later, scrubbing his hair and yawning. Cody shadowed him to the door of a Quonset hut. And after a sufficient period of time had elapsed, followed him inside.

CHAPTER 28

The interior was furnished like an ordinary set of officers' quarters – racks, a steel clothing locker with hanger space, a wardrobe with a mirror. The pilot was examining his face in the mirror and had his back turned when Cody came through the door. He began chatting in Pashtu, obviously accustomed to the presence of a room mate. When Cody stepped up, his reflection visible in the mirror over the pilot's shoulder, the man's shock was sudden and visceral. He whirled, keeping his elbows close to the body, which meant he planned to use them in his counterattack. Anticipating a strike, Cody pistol-whipped him across the jaw, dumping him to the rug.

Moving quickly back to the door, he locked it then stepped over the pilot's body to pull down the blinds of the one window in the room. Then he lifted and dragged the unconscious man to a chair. Settling him with his arms over the back, Cody hunted in the steel clothing locker until locating a belt which he used to secure the pilot's wrists.

There was a sink on the wall. Cody grabbed a water glass, filled it and dashed the contents into the unconscious pilot's face. The man started and came awake with a curse.

"Ai! Yo! You!" He sputtered, blinking angrily. "CIA? Navy SEAL?"

"Just your friendly neighborhood concerned citizen of the Republic, sir." Cody tipped him a mocking salute. "Why don't we start with your name?"

"Fuck you."

"That a family name? Is there an Uncle Fuck You back there somewhere in your history?" Cody dragged over a chair, reversed it and straddled the seat, arms along the back. "Mister, I don't see any point in hurting you. But I don't have a lot of time and I'm about ready to start ripping out fingernails. You'll scream but that won't matter because I'll cut your tongue out before we get started. You'll make these seal-like, croaking noises but that's all. Nothing that will bring anyone running. And by the time I'm done, you'll be missing toes and other body parts so let's just cut out the nonsense and be honest with one another. What's your name, captain?"

The man's head dropped forward onto his chest. He did not speak for a long moment, but when he did, his voice was dead and dull.

"Gul Amran," he muttered. "Late of the Afghan Army Air Force. Now in service to His Excellency, Sheikh Abdul Massoud."

"How many Americans are being held on this base?"

His eyes widened in shock. "You know about that? How you

know about that?"

"How *many*?"

"Five to start. Then they tried to escape. Three are left."

"Held in the shunt-yard? The enclosure there?"

Amran nodded. "Other two are buried in the desert." He held up his hands. "Their bodies were treated respectfully. They were given a proper burial."

"Those Apaches out there in the rows. What kind of shape are they in? Gassed up? Keys in the ignition? All that?"

"The Apaches are kept operational by order of Sheikh Massoud. They are kept gassed up at all times." He smiled. "Apache attack helicopters do not require keys to start."

"Okay. You're going to be my insurance policy. Because we're going to go and get those Americans. And you're going to fly us out of here."

"I see."

"Just do as you're told and no harm will come to you. You have my word."

"We know what the word of Americans is worth!"

"As you wish. But I won't hurt you unless I have to. Now gather up what you need to fly and let's get going."

"I'll need to get my flight vest," said Amran, gesturing toward the bureau.

"Go ahead."

The pilot rose and crossed the room cautiously, keeping his hands raised just above waist level. He gave Cody wide berth. When he stepped in front of the bureau, he gave Cody a reassuring smile in the mirror. Then he opened the top drawer, dug inside and brought out a gun.

Cody reacted the moment he saw steel, launching himself toward the wall and dropping behind the iron bedpost. There was a terrifying, silent scramble as Amran scuttled forward, the pistol outstretched, finger on the trigger but holding off until he had a clear shot. Cody skipped from cover to cover – bed post to steel closet to desk. Then the gun stopped moving and Amran's arm quivered with tension.

Cody whipped out a titanium throwing knife and hurled it with deadly accuracy. It ripped into the pilot's neck, arresting the breath, beginning the bleed, darkening his sight with sure death. But the nerves held on. Amran's finger twitched. And the gun went off.

Cody flung himself again. But the bullet's path was set. It homed in, raked and seared across the top of his left shoulder. Meant for the heart, it cooked the skin. And hurt like almighty hell.

Cody dropped to the rug. Listened.

In the distance, the wail of a siren rose.

They were coming.

In his entire operational life, he had made only sparing use of the emergency pharmacy provided for each agent's use during an insertion mission. Old time agents had carried the lethal 'L' pill, designed to be taken if captured. But operational complexity and pharmacology had advanced considerably since then.

Cody's muscles were going slack, and his vision was darkening. But Langley had planned for such a contingency.

Inside the zippered pouch Cody carried was a blue capsule called a Quanta. With a desperation borne of panic, Cody dug it out and popped it in the final seconds before his vision blurred and shock took him.

Like a switch being flipped, his adrenalin kicked back on and his vision cleared. It was a chemical solution, and one that wouldn't last more than a few minutes. But it should be enough to get him back to the fence and out before the explosions began.

He moved out.

CHAPTER 29

The Quanta took effect as he approached the barracks door. Great waves of energy surged through his body, blurring his vision, causing his hands to twitch as the artificial adrenalin took hold. The stuff was like jet fuel, designed to carry a wounded agent through the crucial minutes of an exfil that might mean the difference between life and death. As these moments now would decide whether or not he reached the Marine enclosure, then the NRF fighters outside.

The room snapped into focus as he put his hand to the knob. In amidst the siren's wail outside, he heard voices. The shot had alerted bystanders, some of whom were coming to investigate.

Cody stepped back around the side of the nearest steel clothing cabinet and drew the Beretta. He heard the Quonset hut door open, took a moment to gauge the pain in his shoulder and marvel at its absence. Then he made the final touches to his plan and waited.

A man in military fatigues appeared, his attention on the

fallen pilot's body. He spun at Cody's presence and opened his mouth to speak. That was when Cody dropped a hand into his pocket and thumbed the detonator trigger, setting off the first chain reaction of explosions.

A quarter-mile away across the base, the Lifesavers roll embedded within a softball-sized wodge of C-4 released a thermal electrical wave into its nest of plastique. The resulting explosion blew off the back end of an old Brezhnev-era T-54 and scattered its insides far and wide in a cloud of shrapnel. Moments later, the tank next to it exploded. And then the one after that.

But by then Cody had shot the man in the Quonset hut and stepped out to shoot his friend in the back as he sprinted out the door. Cody, the effects of the Quanta now leveling out, grabbed and dragged the second man back in across the jamb. Then he locked the door from the inside and pulled it shut as he exited.

Now...

"The Quanta is an experimental amphetamine in the andrenalchrone chemical suite," Cody remembered Dr. Lester explaining during pharmacology orientation. *"Taking one is a risk. But an acceptable one given the ten-minute burst of strength and vitality it will provide even an organism facing catastrophic failure. You agents may need that one day. But beware. Its effects wear off quickly and the danger of ingesting a second dose is exponentially higher. For two minutes' extra burn, you face a 43% likelihood of a cardiac arrest."*

The darkness was crowding the edge of his vision again. He could see it cloaking the enclosure where the Marines were being held. If he moved now...

He would never make it.

His system was failing.

Every fibre in his being impelled him toward the enclosure. He had come *this* far! He *had* to finish! Even if he got mowed down just opening the gate it would be worth it, surely...

But of course, it wouldn't. He was their one asset in-country with knowledge of their location and the ability to stage a rescue. For better or worse, he *had* to stay alive.

So he dropped a second Quanta. The second burst of wind hit him as the next set of chain-reaction explosions began. Then he was sprinting for his break in the fence. Moments later, it seemed, he was creeping out the other side. The first group he saw was a trio of NRF fighters, one of whom recognized him. Cody raised a hand to wave and fell to one knee.

Immediately, there was one on either side of him, lifting. He breathed heavily, coming in and out of consciousness. It was that second damn Quanta, having its way with him. Cody liked a drink now and then but had never been a drug person. He even disliked taking anesthesia for dental procedures. So the amphetamine hit him like a howitzer.

And then suddenly Rashid was there. Cody must have looked more damaged than he felt because the NRF commander's face fell. "Jack Cody," he said in a forlorn tone. "You have been wounded."

Rashid turned and snapped an order to a man behind him. Moments later, one of the desert warriors was kneeling beside Cody and opening a First Aid kit.

"I got shot," Cody said. His perception was stabilizing now that he was lying down. He must have blacked out at the fence because he was now on some sort of stretcher. Or so it seemed. "Shoulder wound."

The Afghan medic peeled a layer of cloth back from Cody's shoulder, leaned in, then turned and spoke to Rashid.

"Memnet says the bullet caused major blood loss. He says you are starting to go into shock."

"I've taken a drug that will keep me conscious," Cody said. "At least for a little while longer."

Outside, the next series of explosions began.

"We have killed many of Massoud's men," Rashid was saying. "We sent a small recon team in to try and get your soldiers, but we got beaten back."

"Thank you for trying." He glanced in the direction of the base. "There are additional explosives in there that have not gone off. We'll save them for now."

"Of course, we –"

At that moment, a shriek split the night somewhere nearby. Then there was a lone pistol shot, followed by a lengthy silence. And then the world exploded.

The canopy of the tent above began to burn. Something like phosphorous was hissing and melting the fabric there. And now machine-gun fire was rising all around them.

Cody drew in a deep breath, rolled from bed and grabbed the nearest weapon he could find – an AK belonging to one of Rashid's men. Then the tent was being torn away by a storm of intruders – men in black. Cody raised the AK to fire just as the blow descended on the back of his head, robbing him of consciousness.

CHAPTER 30

In the Uzbek forward operating base on the Afghan border, Sara Durell pulled off her headphones, rubbed her eyes and looked around. The tiny office of the abandoned airfield she was using had seen better days, like the control tower and the airfield itself. Built during the Soviet-Afghan war, the Uzbek base had been used as a transit hub for shuttle and resupply flights to the front. With the pull-out in 1989, its relevance had diminished to the point at which it was declassified, then downgraded to civilian/courier status and at last shut down. The desk at which Sara sat was a wonder of cultural archaeology. Next to a Vladimir Putin desk calendar were a coaster and ashtray emblazoned with the bold red star of the old USSR.

Yesterday's wars, Sara thought, touching the ashtray. Then she rose, took up her coffee cup and made for the outer office. Markov stood at the coffee table, tiredly lighting a cigarette.

"If you need an ashtray, I've got a commemorative one from the Moscow Olympics," she said, pouring herself a cup. "It's got

Mishka, the Russian bear mascot on it."

Markov laughed. "My uncle was in Soviet army during Olympics. He work security in Olympic village. Soviet Army was having financial problems, so he got paid in free Mishka stuff – bags, cups, hats. Fill his garage with Mishka."

"Maybe he'd care to add an ashtray to his collection?"

Markov was still chuckling when Col. Aripov, Gel. Zinoyev's liaison, joined them.

"We have reports of activity at the base," he said. "Apparently, contact has been made."

Markov checked his watch. "Our drone should be in position now. Let's go check."

Sara and Aripov followed Markov to the small office set aside for his use. The Colonel had laid out his laptop and three cell phones on the desk, one black, one blue and one green. He picked up the green one, hit a speed-dial number and held the phone to his ear. After a brief exchange in Russian, he hung up.

"Drone is entering sector now. We should have pictures soon." He sat at his laptop, clicked on the mouse button and called up a black screen that lightened into an infra-green image of crosshairs. As Sara watched, the crosshairs swiveled, revealing lights below.

An explosion rocked the room, driving Sara forward against the edge of the desk. She folded at the waist, coffee cup flying from her hand. Aripov got slammed against the wall. The chatter of machine-gun fire rose outside. Sara heard voices yelling in Pashtu.

"Markov!" She grasped the edge of the desk and pulled herself upright. "We're under attack! We –"

She broke off, staring down at the crumpled form of the dead Russian. The explosion had driven him against the wall with such force that his head now hung at an unusual angle. His end would have come quickly. His body was all that was left.

Aripov's hand came down on her shoulder. "Come," he said.

They turned and sprinted into the main reception area of the control building. The glass doors had been shredded by the explosion and a handful of Uzbek soldiers lay contorted in death. A row of vehicles, mostly SUVs, were parked with passenger doors facing the terminal. Their attackers were barricaded behind them, taking pot-shots at the force in the lobby.

Aripov quickly took command, barking orders and grabbing up the nearest rifle. Sara snagged an AK from one of the fallen Uzbeks and fell in beside him.

"Josef, Misha and Georgi! Hold the lobby!" he cried in Russian. "Pavel and Leonid, secure the side doors. And you?" He turned to Sara and jerked his head toward the stairs. "Come with me."

Although a Colonel, Aripov was quick to ditch protocol and get his hands dirty. Sara guessed his age at around fifty, but he moved like a fresh recruit, taking the stairs two at a time before turning left.

"This row of offices has windows that look down on the lobby entrance," he said over his shoulder, switching to English for her benefit. "We will mount counterattack from there."

"Sounds good," she replied in Russian. "Taliban?"

"Must be." He raked the slide on his AK. "Come watch me remind them how it was to fight Russian soldiers."

The firing had started up again from downstairs. Aripov

paused before one office door, tried the handle and then took a step back. With a fast kick, he smashed the lock out and charged the door down. It splintered in an oval corona. Aripov pressed through and led the way into the office. A row of windows lined the far wall. Keeping to the shadows, Aripov edged up and peered around. When he turned back, a broad smile edged his beefy face.

"Perfect vantage," he said. He gestured toward a nearby pillar. "You position there. On my signal, open fire."

Sara nodded and took up her position. At Aripov's nod, she darted forward and shouldered open a window. Pushing the snout of the AK forward, she loosed a salvo at the nearest SUV. The bullets raked a path across the vehicle's roof, blowing out glass and shredding metal. The men caught in the blast jigged like marionettes before being cut down. Aripov made swift work of the group beside it.

The Uzbeks in the lobby seized the moment to counterattack. They surged out the front door, guns blazing into the fray. Sara gave them what covering fire she could; the Uzbeks moved too fast and were insanely brave. Two of the four fell. The third group of remaining Taliban leapt into their SUV and roared off, leaving only two men behind.

Sara drew a bead on them and fired. Aripov cried out joyfully as they went down under her bullets, but his jubilation was cut short when one of the fallen managed to bring up his pistol and fire. Two shots: one punched Sara's shoulder, driving her back. The other, a lucky blow, caught Aripov in the skull. Sara emptied her clip into the last shooter as Aripov slid to the ground.

Her firing pin clicked on spent brass.

She was out of bullets.

Silence prevailed.

What the hell?

She fumbled in her pockets for her cellphone, hit the speed-dial for the back-up in Tashkent. The phone flashed: NO SIGNAL.

CHAPTER 31

Cody swam up through layer upon layer of dreams. They broke, scattering like pieces of a shipwrecked boat, leaving behind jumbled thoughts floating aimlessly on the surface of his awareness. Which became voices. Which became a sharp pain in the side of his skull.

He opened his eyes. *Fabric.* Was he in a hospital? He thought maybe. Until he noted the fabric was blue and slightly dirt smeared. A cockroach crept along the outside of the fabric, its silhouette visible in the glare of the lightbulb outside. He seemed to be in some sort of tent. And the voices – those of both men and women – and the sounds of animals and the smell of cooking swirled, stirring the environment. It was dusk. And the voices were speaking in Pashtu.

I'm either a prisoner or the lucky beneficiary of some Good Samaritan, he thought.

He heard footsteps approaching the tent and so pretended to still be asleep. He kept his eyes slitted as the fabric parted and

Shakira stepped into view. Her sudden appearance put things in a whole different light. He opened his eyes and smiled.

"I thought I was dead," he said.

Shakira's face lit up in a big smile. "We are glad to see you are still with us, Jack Cody," she said, kneeling beside the bedroll where he lay, taking his hand in hers. "Your attack on Massoud's base caused much damage. The tribes are all talking about it. Suddenly, the great warlord does not seem so invincible."

"I didn't get the prisoners. Did the NRF...?"

At this, she became somber. "The group you went in with... It was a massacre. They're all dead."

Cody's breath clutched up in his chest. *Dead?* Rashid provided his only radio contact with Sara at the base in Uzbekistan. That left only his phone.

Moving carefully, he patted his pockets. His pack and equipment had been removed but his phone was still snug in its all-weather pocket. He pulled it out and switched it on. The powerful sat-phone operating system relied on military satellites instead of mobile cell towers so getting a signal was no problem. But Sara's unit was shown as off-line. The only trace of her and the team on the border was a single text message:

AIRSTRIKE CONFIRMED FOR DAWN,
2 DAYS FROM NOW. – S.

Dated yesterday.

Cody sat up. "Listen, perhaps someone in the village..."

"We are not in my village, Jack Cody." Shakira bit her lip, suddenly nervous. "I was going to tell you. We are in the desert, in a concealed camp a few miles from Massoud's base."

"So you didn't rescue me?" He brought his feet to the floor and began massaging the back of his neck. "Who did?"

"My fiancé!" Shakira smiled proudly. "That is the right English word, isn't it? *Fiancé*? A man to whom you are promised in marriage?"

"Oh yeah?" Cody smiled. "Congratulations. Who's the lucky guy?"

Just then, the tent flap parted again. Shakira looked up and her grin had the power of a thousand blazing suns. *This must be him,* Cody thought. And suppressed a wave of shock when Tarak Khan entered the tent.

"So!" The bandit leader stopped before Cody and planted his hands on his hips. "The man I fight hand-to-hand in the desert is too tough even for Massoud to kill!" He grinned. "Now I don't feel so bad about losing our duel!"

"You gave as good as you got," Cody allowed.

Tarak Khan laughed. "Shakira will make us tea and we can talk."

It spoke to the reality of Afghan women that had Khan no sooner made the promise on Shakira's behalf than she was bending to gather tea things. Soon a brazier was lit, and an aromatic tea was bubbling, filling the tent with vapor and a rich, spicy odor. Cody guessed this was the 'good tea' they probably kept for guests. Fulfilling the duties of Afghan housewife, Shakira silently prepared and served the tea, then left.

Khan sat examining the tent flap after it closed behind her. "Soon I will marry that fabulous woman, Jack Cody," he vowed. "She comes from a good family – one ordinarily far too good to marry into a bandit clan. But that one has a mind of her own. And a good and loyal heart."

"She is truly remarkable," Cody agreed.

"And you." Khan sipped his tea and examined Cody. "You have come halfway around the world to risk your life to rescue your American soldiers. To me, that is a man worthy of my respect."

"Would you leave any of your own men in the enemy's hands?"

"Of course not." He made a dismissive gesture with one hand. "I wish I had known more about you when we first met. Ordinarily, I might have helped you. But you had Rashid, so we kept our distance."

"Is it true?" Cody examined his tea. "About Rashid and his team?"

"They are all dead." Tarak Khan shook his head. "Those NRF men were a constant irritation to any bandit leader trying to make an honest living. But Rashid was an honorable man, so I respected him. That he brought death to Massoud's men only made me respect him more."

Cody checked his watch. "What time is it?"

"The sun will set soon," Khan replied. He paused, considering Cody's question for a few more seconds before a smile of understanding lit his face. "You intend to go back?"

"Those Marines are still there. And the US Air Force is

going to reduce the base to rubble at dawn tomorrow."

Khan beamed and slapped his knee with an open palm. It was at once a gesture of agreement, approval and support.

"So you will go get them?" he asked.

"Yes. Or die trying."

"That is a man's spirit talking!" Khan rose and pulled Cody to his feet. "Come! I have something to show you."

CHAPTER 32

Cody found his feet and followed Tarak Khan out of the tent. A cooking fire smouldered outside, tended by Shakira who raised a smile at them. Tarak Khan paused and spoke to her in Pashtu. Although Cody could not understand a word of what they said, he could tell from the gentle seriousness of his tone and the gleaming admiration in her eyes that the two were deeply, profoundly, terminally in love. Despite the urgency of his mission, Cody found himself moved by their obvious depth of caring for one another. Such devotion required no translator.

"It is what we fight for," Khan said quietly, leading Cody through the bandit encampment. A cluster of low tents, adorned in desert colors, lay scattered across the mesa, a spiral of smoke rising from the cooking fires lit now that dusk had fallen. Cody heard a giggle and turned in time to see two boys run past him, playing.

"You have children here?" he asked, disbelief plain in his voice.

"Of course!" Khan laughed. "My men have families to feed.

Our women and children travel with us and are useful. Everybody has a job, a purpose. We all work together for the good of the clan." He flashed a secretive smile. "One day, Shakira will leave the house of her aunt and share my tent. She knows how we live and is prepared to join us."

"And you lived like this during the war?"

More laughter. "My friend, we have lived like this for centuries!"

They topped a low dune. Khan put his hand on Cody's shoulder and bid him turn and look back. When he did, he saw a featureless desert, abandoned in the fast-fading dusk. Aside from the wands of smoke rising from the cooking fires, there was no indication of a human habitation anywhere in sight. With the ease of chameleons, the bandits faded into their natural environment with a blend of camouflage and artifice. It occurred to Cody then that the bandits were wild creatures, untamed, ungovernable. He could see why the Taliban and local warlords like Massoud despised them so.

Khan was talking again. "The enemy of my enemy is my friend. Friends help one another, is that not so?"

"That's how it works in America."

"That is how it works here, too." Khan smirked. "Most Americans specialize in fair-weather friendships. They run when the demands become too great. But you." He paused and turned. "You are different."

Cody raised his eyebrows.

Khan seemed to hesitate before speaking. "These Americans Massoud has captured. You know them personally?"

"No."

"Then..." Khan narrowed his eyes, trying hard to understand. "Why have you come? They are not of your family, not of your clan. Why would you come halfway around the world to rescue complete strangers?"

Cody thought carefully before answering.

"In my country," he said, "we are joined not by blood or mutual self-interest. We are united by an agreement – an assent to common ideals. These values mean more to us than anything – more than our own comfort and safety, more than our own self-interest, more than our own lives. Any man who risks his life for those ideals is my brother. My life is a small price to pay for his freedom."

Khan listened. When Cody was done, he shook his head. "That is incredible," he said quietly.

Cody smiled. "It is what we fight for."

* * * * *

Khan led them down the hill to a *wadi* – a dry river-bed – at the bottom of the hill. Cody guessed that this river saw plenty of action during the rainy season; there was ample vegetation lurking at its banks. Khan led them toward a cluster of bushes near a bend. They were of a variety Cody did not recognize, although they resembled thorn bushes. His host grew ever more excited as he approached them.

"The bandit life is different from any other kind of life," he was saying. "The people who stay in one place, who have homes with walls, who are subject to the whims of village elders and mayors – we feel sorry for them. Even though they say of us,

'Oh, those poor impoverished bandits living in the hills with nothing...'" At this, he threw back his head and laughed. "We bandits are free men. And to be free is better than anything!"

"My American brothers in arms would agree."

"So you see? Perhaps we are not so different after all." He stopped by the edge of the bush. "The enemy of my enemy," he repeated quietly, "is my friend."

Then he reached out and grasped something among the branches of the bush. With a sharp movement of his arm, he yanked. The branches of the bush, seared crisp by the season's heat, disintegrated in a cloud of dust. Cody could now see that Khan had grasped a canopy of camouflage netting concealed within the bush.

Whatever's under there has been waiting a long time, he thought. The bandits had draped netting over their prize and then allowed the bush to grow up around it, effectively concealing the thing from even the most probing eyes. And when Khan gave the net another tug, revealing the object in full, he could see why.

Desert-camouflage tan, the looming, formidable, fully armed light tactical vehicle was a state-of-the-art U.S. Army MRAP. Over 12,000 of these Mine-Resistant Ambush Protected vehicles had been deployed in-country – DoD's response to the increased threat of IEDs and ambush.

Cody's surprise must have been evident because Khan laughed. "General Massoud is not the only one to possess war machinery left behind when your country went home!" he said.

Cody checked his watch. "At dawn, he won't have much left. We'll wait until the early morning before going in." He returned his gaze to the MRAP. "That's quite a prize, Tarak."

The bandit leader patted the vehicle affectionately. "Every man should have one! I have only been waiting for the right time to see how she performs. That time has come."

CHAPTER 33

"McKnight. You next. Why did you join up?"

Captivity was starting to wear on the Marines, so Watson had followed her instincts and used her command discretion. She broke from the patterned sequence of duties and meetings she had put together to give Showalter and McKnight a 'barracks day'. Expectations were lifted, discipline was relaxed, and informal talk encouraged. And she remembered Drill Sergeant Cartwright, the man who had inspired her to become a Marine when he visited her high school classroom to give a talk.

"What it takes to command men today," he had said, "is no different from the days of the ancient Romans. A man will follow you if he knows you care about him, about the welfare of his family."

Meaning you can't just crack the whip all the time, Watson thought. She allowed herself to relax a bit, too. But she remained vigilant. And the more she talked with these two guys she didn't really know, the more determined she became to bring them home safely.

Meanwhile, McKnight was considering her question.

"Why'd I join up?" From his place squatting on his haunches, he scratched under the three days' growth of beard lining his jaw and studied wire patterns in the fence. "Time came to pick a trade. I guess. My uncles were in. Fred and Ricky fought in Nam." He shrugged. "Seemed like the family thing to do."

"My grandfather fought in Vietnam," offered Showalter. "A lot of Marines did. The Pacific has been our traditional theatre since World War II. Since even earlier, maybe." He grinned. "What are we doin' here, LT? Don't Marines mean Navy? We got all this beach and no ocean."

Watson and McKnight laughed. She couldn't remember the last time she'd even smiled, let alone laughed. And it felt good.

"What about you, LT?" McKnight looked up shyly to where Watson stood, arms crossed, leaning against a fencepost. "Why did you join?"

"Because I'm a Christian."

"How's that, LT?" Showalter frowned. "Ain't Christianity all about love and forgiveness?"

"It is." She nodded. "But it's also about sacrifice. Marines are the first in. Anywhere. Any time. We take the big risks so the rest of our armed forces don't have to. By projecting force in the service of our nation, we *save* lives. And when we interact with the locals in whatever theatre we find ourselves in, we change lives. Sacrifice is something many people – hell, many *churches* – in our country have forgotten about. But it's fundamental to who we are. I believe that and so I joined."

Watson didn't get to see how McKnight and Showalter reacted, for she looked down at the ground hard. Something inside her was shaken. And she knew in that moment she would give her life for both of them, no questions asked.

And if the chance to get that guy with the sword comes up, I'm gonna take it, she promised herself. *I'm going to kill that son-of-a-bitch.*

✶ ✶ ✶ ✶ ✶

Elsewhere on the base, steel sang and sparks fell in a graceful shower as Abdul Massoud, a.k.a. The Sheikh and 'great imam', sharpened his scimitar against the wheel of a grindstone. He was straddling the grindstone's bench, one sandaled foot pumping the peddle that set the wheel in motion. The primitive machine raised a keening sound that echoed throughout the cavernous airplane hangar in which he sat. Somewhere along the line, the hangar had been emptied. Now it loomed among the buildings on the base like a vast and deserted theater hall. It would suit Massoud's purpose well.

His subaltern Gul entered through a side door and crossed the wide space to stand by Massoud's side. "Great One," he whispered. "I have news."

Massoud paused, half-turned, nodded and spun the wheel twice more before removing his scimitar and resting it across his knee. With a wave of his hand, he bid Gul speak.

"The final representatives of the organizations you have summoned will be here late tonight. As you have instructed, we are making ready to bring samples of the equipment in here for viewing. Our IT man has managed to gain internet access and will be able to track transactions online from our accounts in Zurich and the Bahamas."

"This is very well, and in the nature of things." He drew the scimitar from his knee and balanced it, tip-down, on the ground. "The auction will be lively but go quickly. No one will want to miss out on what we have on offer. You have arranged all the appropriate support?"

"I have, Great One. We will have a table with food, chairs and pillows for sitting, water and tea. Two computer terminals will be brought in here and set up so the brothers who supervise the bookkeeping will witness and verify each transaction. We will post double guards around this building and this end of the base."

"And the prisoners?"

"They have been quiet." Gul shrugged. "They will be unsupervised for an hour or two at most. I foresee no problems, O Great One."

"That is because it is not you but I, Abdul Massoud, founder of The Way, to whom it has been given to lead Islam from barbarism to the light of a new Golden Age. Such a task is not fit for the likes of you, unfit even to understand these Americans and the threat they pose to *altariqa,* to The Way. Their presence is an infection."

"Yes, Great One."

"Choose one." Massoud took up his blade and ran a thumb along its edge. "Bring him to me at dawn tomorrow. It's time to cull the herd."

CHAPTER 34

Onboard the flight deck of the USS *Ronald Reagan,* Captain Elijah Browne braced his shoulders against the wind of the Indian Ocean and walked the row of F-35 Stealth combat strike fighters lined up on deck. The crew chief, spotting Browne's silhouette as he approached, snapped to attention and saluted.

"We five-by-five?" Browne asked crisply, returning the salute and examining the row of jets illumined in the dark by the carrier's halogen running lights.

"All birds are green light for wheels-up! Just give us the word, sir!"

"Excellent. Thank you, chief."

Firing off another salute, Browne slipped through a hatch in the deck tower and quickly descended the metal stairs to the below-decks companionway. A group of enlisted men crowding the corridor spotted him, immediately made a hole and stepped aside as he passed. Those wearing their covers saluted. All drew sharp inhales of relief as he passed.

"That's him," Browne heard one whisper. *"That's the Iceman..."*

He grinned bitterly. He hadn't chosen the nickname for himself. But he liked it.

It suited him.

Coming to the ready-room doorway, he knocked twice and entered. His crew of five men – one for each of the other F-35s now on deck – snapped to attention as their commander entered. The six of them would crew the half-dozen jets slated for the operation, each F-35 representing the bleeding edge of US combat aviation technology.

"Take your seats." Browne moved to the head of the table, removed his cap and flight jacket and laid them on a chair. Taking up a remote control, he fired up the PowerPoint he'd prepared for the meeting.

"This carrier is currently hosting a team of US Army Delta Force operators," he began. "They are here to facilitate extraction of US military personnel currently being held prisoner at our target site, designated Omega-1. This rescue is codenamed Operation REDEMPTION."

The screen faded into a satellite picture of the abandoned French base in the Panjshir Valley.

"Omega-1 is an abandoned French military base constructed in the early days of Operation ENDURING FREEDOM. Our French allies used it to coordinate military operations in the Panjshir Valley, most involving armored and air force units. So it's a big base." Browne clicked a button on the remote and the picture was replaced by a close-up. Clearly visible: runways and airport buildings.

"The French abandoned Omega-1 a few years ago. They leased it to Uncle Sam for a while until we had no more use for it. Then we moved on. So it's been lying there literally abandoned for three years. That is...until this guy found it."

Click. An image of Abdul Massoud appeared.

"This ugly son-of-a-bitch is Abdul Massoud. He's the founder of a Taliban splinter group known informally as 'The Way'. He's a player – a warlord and major bad news. Imagine a cross between Charles Manson, Saddam Hussein and Jim Jones. A real psychopath. And he's managed to amass the following abandoned ordnance and secure it on the base."

Click. A list of abandoned US military equipment filled the screen.

One of the airmen let out a low whistle.

Browne's glare shot in the direction of the sound. "You have something to add, Stevens?"

"Sir, that's a helluva' lot of stuff!"

A low chuckle passed among the pilots.

Browne gave a sour smirk. "That's not exactly a unit of measurement we use in the Navy. But it'll do. Massoud has indeed amassed a huge stockpile of weapons suitable to mount major military operations in theatre. Our job?"

Click. A map projection showing the Indian Ocean and environs as well as the *Reagan's* current position.

"The Deltas are scheduled to be deployed and back by zero hour, when we will scramble from the *Reagan* and proceed north."

Click. Arrows appeared, showing the squadron's projected flight path.

"We will breach Pakistani airspace within minutes. At which point we drop to minimum altitude and hit the afterburners. We will be in and out of their country before they know it. Our pickets will move forward once we approach the Afghan border and intercept any welcoming committee. We do not expect top-of-the-line opposition, but we intend to be ready just in case. Pickets will eliminate any combat air cover as we come in-country. Then we climb to bombing altitude and proceed to target. Estimated flight time is twenty-two minutes."

Click. A list of the ordnance secured for their use during the mission appeared.

"This is a saturation bombing run. We will proceed in successive waves, wiping out buildings and equipment recursively. Group A will strike, followed by Group B which will hit the same target as Group A before Group A leapfrogs them for the next leg. We will proceed in this way: A bombs, B re-bombs and then A leapfrogs to the next sector. As you can see..." He swept a hand at the munitions list. "We're giving them the full meal deal. Catastrophic concussion, superheating and a resulting firestorm. *Nothing* on that base will be left alive, standing or even remotely usable. And any living organism within a mile will get the air sucked out of its lungs."

He put down the remote, leaned forward over the table and concluded:

"Total scorched Earth. Nothing left standing. After the Del-

tas are done, we go in fast, hit our marks and get the hell home.
I aim to bring in all my ships. Questions?"

No one stirred.

"We go in four hours." Browne checked his watch. "Grab
some rack time."

* * * * *

After the last of his pilots had filed out, Browne returned to the
companionway and took the steps up two at a time to the captain's quarters. The Marine guarding the captain's door turned,
knocked twice and admitted Browne. In the sitting room,
the *Reagan's* skipper conferred with a rear-admiral. Browne
stepped in, came to attention and saluted.

The rear-admiral looked up. "Air crew standing by?"

"Sir, birds are on the flight line. Air crew is briefed and
ready."

"Excellent. At ease, Captain Browne." The rear-admiral took
up a file folder and opened it. "Some additional info, Captain.
Your ears only. The Deltas are scrambling to back up a CIA
special warfare team already operating in-country. REDEMP-
TION is a pick-up job. They move in and grab our people right
before your team hits."

"And if REDEMPTION is unsuccessful, sir? Do we abort?"

"Negative." The rear-admiral shook his head. "You follow
your orders to the letter regardless of whether or not our people are out. The Commander-in-Chief wants that base leveled.
So let's just pray to God whoever the CIA has on the ground
knows what the hell he's doing."

CHAPTER 35

In the early pre-dawn hours, the MRAP crept through the chaos of rock, sand, dry riverbeds and canyons that separated the bandit camp from Massoud's base. Cody rode up front with Tarak Khan. In back he knew were Khan's heavily armed bandit warriors, locked and loaded and ready to rain hellfire down on the enemy. One even carried a flame-thrower. They were arguably some of the most unusual allies with whom Cody had ever gone into battle. Yet he felt oddly reassured.

These guys don't have SOPs, formal orders or milestone objectives, he thought. *But they work together instinctively, have unity of purpose and a common faith and creed...*

Those things made up for a multitude of operational sins.

"Time from here to base is one hour," Tarak Khan said, eyes never leaving the windshield as he spoke. "We pass through interesting tourist attraction. Ancient village. Here since days of Alexander the Terrible."

"Viewing tourist attractions isn't high on my list of operational objectives…"

The bandit leader threw back his head and laughed, down-shifting as he guided the MRAP over a low hill.

"And… 'Alexander the Terrible.' Why do you call him that?"

Cody saw Tarak's jawline firm.

"You know who last western man to capture Afghanistan was, Jack Cody?"

"Who?"

"Alexander." The bandit leader's eyelids drooped to half-mast. "Many came after. The Hindus. The Romans. The British. The Russians. You Americans… All failed! But not Alexander. He became warlord of all Afghanistan. You know how? I tell you how, Jack Cody. Alexander come to village. He slaughter every man, woman and child. Then move onto next village. And so on and so on. For two years. He was not brilliant, great man. He was not master tactician or grand imperialist. To us, Jack Cody, he was the angel of death that blew over our villages, our land."

"And this is why you fight?"

"And this why we fight." Tarak Khan nodded firmly, squared his shoulders and re-applied himself to guiding the MRAP through the bleak terrain.

The landscape rose and fell before them. The vehicle's lights, designed for complex operational variables, had numerous settings. Khan had wisely chosen the 'glow' option, spearing as little light as possible into the terrain ahead. But it made navigation a slow, painstaking process. Fortunately, Khan was a natural. They made solid progress for another quarter hour until the silhouettes of ruined buildings loomed ahead.

"There." Khan's voice held a reverent note. "Is Tajool."

Cody scanned the ruins ahead through his infra-green bin-oculars. From here, the structures appeared to be no different from the wattle and daub structures of Shakira's village. But Khan had spoken of their antiquity. He noted breaks in walls, collapsed roofs, empty lots where buildings had obviously once stood. Someone had cut through this sector of Panjshir with the precision of a buzz-saw.

"Is that Alexander's work?" he asked.

Tarak Khan bit his lips. And nodded.

Cody could not help but feel a sense of the past haunting him as Tarak guided the MRAP toward the place. He imagined legions of Macedonian hoplites, shields and spears trained, advancing on the same position. *Because the buildings and the vegetation can change,* he thought. *But throughout time, terrain stays more or less the same.*

Tajool was a tactical prize, he realized. Situated at the cen-ter of a more or less level plain, it commanded the road to the heights that, in turn, commanded it. *No army could ever get through here without holding this village,* he realized. Now or in the ancient past.

The globes of light pressed forward in the dark. Cody saw a curve in the road, the blasted edge of what might once have been a house, then an opening into something like a town square. With...

"Tarak, is that a fountain?"

"Yes, Jack Cody. In ancient times, these places flowed rich

with water. Forests of palms. And good farmland."

"This could be a good fallback position," Cody said. "We could rendezvous back here in the event we get separated."

"My thoughts exactly, Jack Cody." Tarak was nodding vigorously. "We can also stash additional weapons and ammunition in case."

Cody smirked. He liked the way this guy thought. "Okay, then. How about there?" He pointed. "That large building with the roof and part of the front wall blown out? It's facing toward the base. And the remaining wall offers a redoubt."

"Perfect!" Tarak clapped his hands, re-grasped the wheel and steered the MRAP in that direction.

At his bidding, and under his supervision, the warriors in the rear disembarked and formed a human chain to pass weapons and boxes of ammunition from hand-to-hand to be stashed in the ruin. Cody remained in the passenger seat. It occurred to him to try Sara again at the border base. He produced his cell and tried, but again received no reply.

Something's up.

He opened the door and stepped from the MRAP. The line was continuing to move equipment and ammo. All seemed well. Until it didn't.

A rattle of machine-gun fire erupted from the nearby buildings. Cody drew his Beretta and hit the ground.

CHAPTER 36

"We're four minutes out!"

The Delta Force captain watched his crew acknowledge their comprehension with thumbs up, then returned his attention to the data tablet. The online GPS and digital read-out provided real-time data on mission status and allowed him to remain in contact with mission command onboard the *Reagan*.

They had been airborne for more than an hour, the heavy Chinook chopper carrying not just the team itself but three quads for use in navigating the desert terrain. The first leg of their trip was through Pakistan and then over the border to a landing zone within striking distance of their mission target, Omega-1. Intel confirmed their LZ was in an area of the country with almost no Taliban oversight. Once there, they would disembark and stage up for their journey to exfiltrate the captured Marines and their CIA rescuers.

"Beginning our descent." The chopper pilot's voice crackled in the Delta captain's earphones.

"Starting the mission clock," replied the Delta commander. "How we looking?"

"We're out in the sticks. Last time this place saw any military action was when Alexander the Great was here."

* * * * *

Cody returned fire. How long had they been out there, lurking in the shadows before attacking? He heard Tarak's voice raised, the bandit leader shouting orders to his men. He heard them moving forward through the rubble to engage the enemy. More gunfire. Then another sensation... Wind...

Cody felt the helicopter before he heard it. The pressure from the prop wash hit him seconds before the thrumming. Then he was looking up at a Chinook transport chopper lowering itself through the night air toward the town.

That's got to be ours, he thought. Sara had mentioned special forces were inbound. But given the circumstances, their timing could not have been worse.

Tarak Khan rushed up beside him. "Jack Cody, give me one reason I should not shoot that down!"

"Because they're probably American! Probably here as mission back-up!"

"Then we create space!"

The bandit leader rushed off to move his men back. Cody rummaged in his pack for a flare. He fired two shots toward the mysterious enemies' position, then rose and sprinted toward the Chinook's intended landing zone. They were coming down in a wide-open space behind the first row of houses, a sort of sandy clearing. Cody moved out to the edge of the clearing, waved the flare back and forth three times before planting it in the ground and withdrawing to a safe distance.

That was when the unseen enemy opened fire on the Chinook.

Tracers erupted from between the buildings. Cody spun and offered covering fire. From here he had a better perspective on the enemy force and numbered them at around six. Khan's force was larger, as was likely the force in the Chinook. But these six had been enough to cause trouble for them both.

The chopper absorbed two shots before the pilot cut short the landing and hovered. More gunfire: Cody tamped it down for them and let the bird come in for a touch-down. No sooner had the wheels hit the ground than a fresh burst erupted from the houses. It was answered a few seconds later by Tarak's men. *Good,* Cody thought. The bandits had come up and engaged the enemy from behind.

The Chinook's massive tail ramp was lowering, throwing a shaft of light. Cody went by the flare he had planted and knelt, following the protocol for unexpected encounters with other special forces in the field: let them see you, assume a non-threatening posture and wait for them to engage. As the ramp touched down, two quads manned by black-clad Delta operators buzzed out and conducted wide flanking maneuvers to either side of their attackers. The remaining Deltas came out in bursts of three and four. During the last one, the mission commander sprinted to take a knee beside Cody.

"You our CIA guy?"

"That's me. We had no idea you were staging up here. Sorry about the reception committee."

"Any idea who they are?"

"None. Only that there are about six and they're persistent. I'm here with friends – locals. They're engaging the enemy from the rear."

"Roger that." The Delta leader hit the transmit switch on his comms unit. "Ranger One, Ranger Two…enemy being engaged by friendlies. Repeat, engaged by friendlies. Watch your crossfire." He cocked his head for the response, nodded once, the returned his attention to Cody.

"We're inbound to the base now," said Cody. "But we'll stay and help you mop up your LZ."

A sudden shriek rose from the ruined village as a streak of fire from the flamethrower found and engulfed an enemy position. Cody doubted they'd learn much from the remains.

"Go make contact with your friends," the Delta leader said. "We'll advance from here and meet you in the middle!"

"Roger that!"

Cody waited for a break in the action before sprinting the distance to the edge of the nearest ruin. He was swaddled in shadow, armored behind stone and completely invisible to anyone. He had the perfect vantage from which to track enemy movement. He began noting the location of muzzle flashes. And as he did, his regard for the enemy force only grew.

These guys are good, whoever they are, he thought. Their battlefield discipline, economic use of fire, changing locations

– all pointed to seasoned operators.

But so were the Deltas. He saw them advancing now and could tell from the fire approaching from the opposite direction that Khan's bandits had isolated the group within the open area with the ancient fountain – one from which perhaps Alexander himself had taken a drink, back when this land was fertile with rivers and crops instead of landmines and blood.

Slowly, the gunfire trickled off. He heard voices, pleas of surrender in...

What? He frowned. *No, it can't be...*

Cody rushed past the buildings separating him from the enemy. He arrived to find Khan holding four men at gunpoint. His bandits and the Deltas stood on the outskirts watching. The men Khan covered were on their knees, hands behind their heads. The bodies of their comrades lay stacked nearby.

And that's when he realized it was true. The pleas of surrender *had* been in Russian. And had come from these guys, who were obviously anything but local.

"Who are you?" Cody snarled, stepping up to the nearest one.

"Russian military contractors. We are with Black Eagle Corporation." The man grinned, exposing a row of pearly white teeth that had a few missing. "Who are you guys?"

CHAPTER 37

"Kill them!"

Cody shot a glance at Tarak Khan who stood, tensed and glaring, pistol extended at the end of a trembling arm as he covered the Russian mercs.

"Russian scum! Murderers! Kill them!"

Cody and the Delta commander shared a glance. This wasn't in the mission brief.

"Tarak." Cody spoke softly. "No."

"Why *not?*" The bandit leader's tone was frantic. "Russians slaughtered thousands of civilians in our territory! Caused untold misery! They should pay!"

"Russians thirty years ago, maybe." Cody stepped forward and laid a hand on the bandit leader's arm. "These men had nothing to do with it. They weren't even born when it happened. Let it go."

Khan's jaw firmed, teeth grinding on teeth as he fought down his own impulses. Cody felt for the guy. He felt for any of the Afghan locals, to be honest, whether they had suffered under Coalition or Russian hands.

This damn country's been through the wringer, he thought. History had been impartial and unbiased in its apportioning of misery.

At length, Khan relented. He lowered the arm holding the pistol and turned to Cody. "Because you ask, Jack Cody. But only because you ask."

"Fair enough." Cody turned to the Delta commander. "Your call. What do we do with them?"

"We'll hold them." The Delta chief put two of his guys on the task of securing the Russians with a nod. "I'm leaving a guy back here to secure the landing zone, anyway. We'll zap-strap and duct tape our Russian military contractors until we're done, then release them prior to dust off."

"Works for me," said Cody. He turned to Khan. "We'll proceed with our mission and use this point as a fall-back if necessary. Like we planned."

"This is good, Jack Cody." Tarak Khan nodded.

"We're supposed to wait for a signal from base to go pick you up," said the Delta leader. "But you said you can't reach your contact in Uzbekistan?"

"Radio silence for hours, now," Cody said, and tried hard not to worry about Sara.

"Here." The Delta leader reached into his pack and produced two flares. "Here's one blue and one yellow. Once you've re-leased the POWs set off the blue one and we'll move in. If you encounter trouble, fire the yellow and we'll recon and reassess."

Under the circumstances, it was as workable a plan as they were likely to conceive. Cody and Tarak agreed.

It didn't take the Delta team long to secure the remaining mercs. They carried black plastic zap-straps and masking tape in their kit for just such an eventuality. The four Russians were secured with their hands tied behind their backs, their mouths taped over, and set with their backs against one wall of a ruined dwelling. One of the Deltas remained on post to cover them while Cody and the commander went to the Chinook.

"I'm going to hook you up with one of our spare comms rigs," the commander said. "Won't get you as far as Uzbekistan but it'll keep you in contact with us. If worse comes to worst, you can relay a message to your people via our 'net."

Cody accepted the transmitter in its black strap harness. About the size of a mobile phone, it had an effective range of thirty miles and was equipped with a headset and floater mike. Cody tried them on and did a test transmission. The Delta commander listened at his own headphones, nodded and gave a thumbs up.

"I'll signal once I reach the base," Cody said.

"Sounds good," said the commander.

"Red One, this is Red Scout... I have contact in-bound."

The Delta commander's finger flew to his transmit switch. "Red One, stand by. We're en route."

Cody followed the Delta commander as he double-timed it back to his team. At the outer edge of their assembly point, one of the Deltas had taken a knee and was scanning the western approach with something like a computer tablet.

"It's a helo, sir." The Delta sounded sure. "No military designator. In-bound and should be here in minutes."

The Delta commander turned to Cody. "You and your guys should go. Clear out before that helo arrives. We'll handle it, whatever it is."

"You sure?"

"Yeah." The Delta waved a hand. "We've got this. Go. Get your guys."

Cody and Tarak shared a glance. He could tell the bandit leader was reluctant to abandon these new allies. But if their mission was to succeed, they had to get back on the trail.

"Okay," said Cody. He shook the Delta commander's hand. "Good luck."

"Stay safe."

Tarak Khan gave the signal and his men scattered back to the MRAP. Within moments, he and Cody were hauling themselves into the cab. The bandit leader started up the truck and began edging forward along the main street of the village.

"We'll go without lights, Jack Cody," he said. "Until we are clear."

"Good idea."

The thrum of the approaching chopper was audible now, swallowing the night sounds, flattening and scattering features of terrain with its prop wash. Cody saw the glare of its spotlight gleam in the rear-view mirror an instant before its rockets began firing.

Khan threw on the brakes and twisted around the look back.

The helicopter – black, unmarked – was hovering now and firing missile after missile into the remains of the village. As Cody watched, the Chinook exploded in a ball of flame.

The Deltas were gone. His link to Sara was gone.

That was it.

They were on their own.

CHAPTER 38

For a long moment, Cody sat stunned. As the flames from the explosions rippled in the rear-view mirrors and lit up the sky, he kept asking himself the same question over and over until it burst from his lips.

"Who the hell *was* that?" He craned around in his seat to watch the receding village. "Was that Massoud's guys?"

"No, Jack Cody." Tarak Khan downshifted and steered the MRAP into a dry riverbed. "Chopper came from the east. Massoud's base is west of here."

"Taliban? No." Cody thought. "They must be connected to our Russian friends."

"If they are here, it is for Massoud." Khan sounded convinced. "NRF fighters are controlled from Uzbekistan, and they do not use mercenaries. Is point of honor. And certainly, the Taliban will not."

"So they were here looking for work." Cody laid a hand on Khan's arm and jerked his head at the rear view. "Wait."

Khan applied the brakes and studied the image in the mirror. In a second, he saw what Cody had seen – that the black helicopter had finished up with the village and was turning away from the flames and wreckage. Its spotlight moved, twisting through the arc of its rotation until it pointed slightly ahead and straight down. Then it began moving ahead at a fly-crawl.

"They're following our tracks."

At this Khan grinned fiercely. "They seek to eliminate the tribal vermin, hey? Come, Jack Cody. Let me show you how true sons of Afghanistan fight."

Khan spun and hammered on the panel separating the cab from the truck bed. Cody heard the back doors of the MRAP open and the sound of men disembarking. The man with the flamethrower appeared at Khan's window. Khan issued a series of clipped orders and pointed into the desert. The man with the flamethrower nodded, called to the rest of the group and began hiking away through the scrub. Cody noticed how the men dragged their feet, kicking up huge clouds of dust and leaving a slew of tracks.

"You like fruit?"

"Uh, sorry?"

Khan bellowed laughter and opened the driver's side door, slipping down to the sand. Cody followed him around to the back of the MRAP. The chopper was closer now, its spotlight a burning presence, hanging in the sky like a flaming angel. Within another few minutes, it would find the MRAP.

Khan ducked into the rear of the vehicle and emerged soon holding a Stinger missile launcher. "We are honored guests at the wedding feast!" he crowed. "See?" He shook the launcher. "We have the orange! Come on!"

Khan kept to the edge of the MRAP, and Cody followed. Reaching a section of flat rock that jutted from the sand, the bandit leader followed it. His path took him in the opposite direction of his men. Cody kept up, careful not to leave any tracks.

He's fast for a big guy, Cody thought. Tarak hustled through the scrub and scree with a jackrabbit's ease. He brought them to the top of a small rise and paused.

"There." He pointed. "My men are over there."

The burning halogen spotlight on the chopper's nose had reached the dry riverbed. It hovered off to Cody's left, nosing the air to either side as if trying to pick up a scent. It paused, as though finding something, then its nose tilted downward and the chopper crept forward, following the tracks of the MRAP.

"This is Russian mind at work," observed Khan. "Americans are ruthless and creative. Russians? Ruthless and plodding. Which would you rather face?"

Cody smirked but said nothing.

Out in the darkness, a pinpoint of light appeared. Cody recognized the beam of a laser pointer. He shot a look back at the chopper. The beam had been so brief and so low that it had gone unnoticed by the pilot.

"My men are in position." Khan's voice swelled with satisfaction. "What comes next is easy. Like stealing an orange from a baby."

"In America, we say candy."

"Hm. That is why Americans are so overweight." Khan shouldered the Stinger and grinned.

A distance away, the chopper was creeping up on the parked MRAP with its open rear doors. Soon it had the vehicle fixed in its spotlight. Cody heard the gun mounts on the aircraft swivel into position. A moment later light was stabbing down through the air, framing the MRAP in its glare. The chopper lowered itself slightly, the pilot seeking a vantage from which to study the truck and the light intensified and the prop wash blew sand and rocks around in a mini-twister.

"That's it," Khan whispered. "Now take the bait, Ivan."

The spotlight stabbed down on the area beside the MRAP – a stretch of sand muddled by footprints. Again, it nosed side-to-side, adjusting its altitude and spotlight. Then it set off, following the tracks.

Machine-gun fire blazed up from the dark desert. Bullets struck and bounced from the helicopter's armor plating and the pilot, sensing the direction of fire, turned. A moment later, his own guns blazed. And Khan laughed.

"But your own men?" Cody asked.

"My men are no longer there." The bandit leader flipped up the Stinger's sights and activated the firing sequence. "These are trained mountain fighters, Jack Cody. More than a match for a big, stupid, plodding Russian bear."

The chopper stopped firing, re-oriented itself and moved further into the desert. Within moments, it was directly across from their position.

Khan was whispering now, one eye closed, the other squinting through the sites as he positioned the Stinger. The scream of the helicopter's motors filled the sky. Gunfire chittered from among the dark rocks and sand below.

"In the name of Allah, the compassionate and the merciful," Khan whispered. His fingers hit the fire control switch and the Stinger roared to life, its heat-seeking rocket swishing across the dark valley to strike the chopper and reduce it to a blazing ball of burning metal.

CHAPTER 39

"Mr. President?"

President Harwood looked up from his desk in the White House residence. A Secret Service agent hovered in the doorway.

"Sir, the Chief of Staff is here with the Chairman of the Joint Chiefs. They're asking for a moment of your time."

"Send them in." Harwood plucked off his reading glasses and dropped them on the stack of budget paperwork before him. Congress was calling to changes for the next fiscal year and wading through the resulting paperwork was onerous. He welcomed the distraction.

Corbett entered, the Chairman close behind him. Harwood could sense their worry as he rose and gestured for them to take a seat with him before the fireplace. A chill seized his heart. He felt certain Operation REDEMPTION was the source of their concern.

"Mr. President, thank you for seeing us." Corbett and the Chairman exchanged a look before the Chief of Staff continued. "We've just had word from the *Reagan*."

"And?"

"It's not good, sir." The Chairman sat forward on the couch. "The Delta team lifted off for its staging area near the target. Shortly afterwards, mission planners lost contact with the team. We sent a drone in for a fly-over."

Corbett laid pictures out on the desk. Harwood leaned forward to study the images. Shot at night through infrared cameras, the photo was indistinct in places. But showing clearly dead-center was the strewn wreckage of a large helicopter.

"We've confirmed that's the chopper that brought the Deltas in. It appears the team has been attacked and their chopper compromised. Their immediate whereabouts and status are unknown."

Harwood's jaw firmed. "Nothing via radio contact?"

"No, sir."

The President sighed and sat back. "Then we have no choice but to assume they've been totally compromised."

A long silence settled.

"Sir," said Corbett after a time, quietly. "We're going to have to proceed with the airstrike. Possibly with our people in the line of fire."

"Understood." Harwood rose. "Give the order. We go, regardless of other concerns."

As the two men thanked him and left, Harwood's thoughts

turned to Jack Cody.

"It's all up to you now, Jack," he said quietly. Then he bowed his head in prayer.

* * * * *

Onboard the *Reagan*, Captain Elijah Browne presented himself at the door to the captain's quarters. The Marine guard knocked, announced Browne's arrival and let him pass. Browne entered the sitting room area, where the captain conferred with the rear-admiral.

"You wanted to see me, sir?"

The rear-admiral's expression was dark. He took one last glance at the file in front of him before closing it and turning to Browne.

"Captain Browne. I regret to inform you that the Delta Force mission has been gravely compromised. We now know that their chopper has been destroyed and their radio communications have gone silent. We have no choice but to assume they have all been either captured or killed."

The force of this news struck Browne like a falling rock. He swallowed, steadied himself and said: "I'm sorry, Admiral. That's terrible news."

"Indeed, it is." The rear-admiral rose and walked to a porthole. He gazed through at the dark sea beyond. "Those Americans held prisoner at the base now have only the CIA's team in-country to help them. There's a chance they may be rescued.

But then again..."

He trailed off.

"We'll have drones on station an hour before your squadron arrives. And we'll see what we can see. But." He turned and speared Browne with a hard glance. "Captain, I need to know your pilots are ready to go in there and bomb that place regardless of whether or not our people are still present."

"Yes, sir. Absolutely. One hundred percent. To the man."

The rear-admiral was nodding now. "God knows, I wish it didn't have to be this way."

"Me too, sir," said Browne.

"That will be all."

"Thank you, Admiral. Captain."

Browne turned and left to join his squadron.

* * * * *

In the silent, sinister, wee hours before dawn, Kendra Watson sat awake, worrying, as McKnight and Showalter snored peacefully nearby.

All her life she had faced and surmounted obstacles. Whether in school, church, jiu-jitsu class or Marine basic training, she had always risen to the challenge. She knew that one of the biggest obstacles one faces in life is oneself. And so for that reason, she had cultivated a personal self-confidence that was steely and uncompromising. She was not so naïve as to believe that she was invulnerable. But she knew it was crucial to hide her doubts and fears from the men she led. Because subordinates expect confidence in a commander. Anything less leads to doubt. And that can get Marines killed.

She studied McKnight and Showalter.

This may be my last command, she thought. *It could all end for us here, in this shitty desert, murdered by these brutal assholes. I have to face that possibility and be ready for it. I have to keep up a brave front and show confidence for my men. I have assumed the burden of command and all it requires. I must lead them. If necessary, unto death.*

A tear rolled down her cheek, unbidden. She scrubbed it away angrily.

Get yourself under control, girl!

She thought of her family, of her mother and father and her grandmother who lived with them. Her grandmother, the solid old matriarch who attended Catholic Mass daily, who worked her fingers to the bone, constantly cooking and cleaning and caring for all of them. Grandmother, who never complained, never took a day off sick and who never failed to have a word of stern encouragement or kind admonishment exactly when it was needed most.

Grandmere, you were always there for me. For all of us...

And it came clear to her then. She must follow her grandmother's example. Be the strong and uncomplaining backbone of this little crew. And face whatever sacrifices awaited her. For she knew that to command is, above all, to serve.

Her men were resting.

Their plan was set, and each knew his role.

They would make their break when their guard came to do his pre-dawn check.

Nothing left to do now but follow Grandmere's example, she thought. And bowed her head in prayer.

CHAPTER 40

The MRAP crawled through the desert, closing in on the base. Cody sat forward in the passenger seat, gripping the dash and squinting into the gloom. The globes of light thrown by the headlamps barely cut the thick darkness ahead. Although Tarak Khan seemed to know exactly where he was going, Cody wasn't taking any chances. The road ahead was treacherous and the desert, full of risk. He hadn't come this far only to be ambushed by a few missteps so close to his objective. The jets would soon be warming up on the *Reagan's* flight deck. Time was short.

And so he was the first to spot the debris scattered in the *wadi* ahead. At first, he thought his eyes were deceiving him. But a few blinks and a lot of squinting soon convinced him that what he was seeing was real.

"Is that a...bicycle?"

Tarak Khan threw on the brakes, killed the headlights and waited for his eyes to adjust to the gloom. There was just enough moonlight to glimmer off the edges of the objects in the sand ahead.

"Is bicycle," Khan said. "Is mountain bicycle."

"Stay here."

Cody slipped out of the passenger side door and crouched low, keeping to the shadows. In the moonlight were two sets of tracks, single grooves in the sand. He recognized the tread pattern of thick mountain bike tires. He and Tarak had been on the lookout for picket sentries, but it had never occurred to him that perhaps Massoud had seen fit to equip them with mountain bikes.

But that doesn't make sense, Cody thought. *Tribal and traditional dress codes would make operating a bike difficult if not impossible under the best of conditions. But this…?*

He crept ahead, eyes on the triangular frame of the bike as he approached. The thing had been upended and stuck seat-down in the sand. One wheel twisted lazily in its socket. The other had been removed. The chain hung slack in its casing. And then twenty feet further, he saw another bike: this one lying on its side. And there was more.

He saw an open backpack on a flat rock. A spill of clothing fell from its open mouth, splayed across the rock. An emptied water bottle, its cap loose, lay close by. He heard voices…

Moving forward, he dropped to hands and knees and crawled the low rise. Reaching the top, he peered over.

A half-dozen men stood in a circle, shoving a woman around in their midst. One of the men punctuated the shoving with a lecture in a high-pitched falsetto, breaking off every now and then to whinny a high-pitched giggle of laughter. The woman was dressed in bike shorts and a sports top. From the awkwardness of her stance and occasional stumble, Cody could tell she was wearing bike shoes. Another man, similarly attired, lay on his back a short distance away, obviously unconscious.

He crept back to the MRAP.

"Two mountain bikes. Clothing and camping equipment. Looks like a group of locals has waylaid the bicyclers and knocked the male unconscious. They're roughing up the woman while one of them utters this godawful laugh…"

At this, Tarak's eyebrows jumped. "Group of local men, you say? This laugh. Is giggling? High? Like a girl's?"

"Yeah!" Cody was surprised.

Tarak growled, shaking his head. "Amwar!"

"Who?"

"Local bandit. Small time guy." Tarak opened the driver's side door. "Him and his gang, they are like rats in my territory. Bothering villagers. Stealing petty things. Being assholes. Jack Cody, these bicyclers. They are white, like you?"

"Seems so, yeah."

"Is stupid place to go for bicycle trip!" Tarak had slipped a pistol out from his robes. Cody recognized the sleek silhouette of a classic Walther PPK as the bandit leader screwed a silencer into place on the weapon.

"Extreme tourism." Cody shook his head. "I've bumped into it before. Well-to-do Westerners who are bored in their condos in London or New York so get a thrill backpacking or bicycling through warzones."

"Backpacking?"

"Putting on a pack and hiking around for a couple of days in the middle of nowhere."

"Is stupid!" The bandit chieftain flung a hand in disgust. "Tarak Khan would give much to live a quiet life in a nice big western city with plenty of money! Jack Cody, if I had a fortune, I would have nice apartment on Madison Avenue and never leave!"

"Well, you've led a hard life compared to them..."

"Probably so. Come."

Cody let Khan lead the way. With surprising agility, the bandit chief advanced to the top of the rise and lay prone. Cody moved in beside him.

The woman was still upright, but her white top had been ripped. She was struggling to hold the torn section up across her breasts as the men continued to shove and grope at her. She uttered a strange, breathy sound that Cody recognized as failed attempts at screams. She was scared, out of breath and desperate.

Khan's face grew thunderous.

"This is not how true Muslim men behave, Jack Cody." Khan's voice held a brittle anger that was intense in its softness. "It is said among true believers that a woman must never be beaten. Not even with a flower."

Then he raised and leveled the Walther. And fired off a shot.

CHAPTER 41

Sara Durell slumped in the radio operator's chair, the bullet wound in her shoulder burning as she struggled to formulate a plan.

The radio was a dead loss, shot to bits in the attack. The Taliban raid had proven as devastating as it was unexpected. A cross-border suicide mission, to be sure. But devastating, nonetheless.

How the hell did they pull it off? She checked the bandage on her shoulder. *And – what's more to the point – why?*

The Taliban were violent and brutal. They even possessed a rudimentary sort of battlefield discipline. They had proven that they could stage and mount military operations of considerable size. But for the most part they tended to remain in their own neighborhood. You didn't hear about their fighters conducting raids into adjoining nations. When it came to killing, they preferred to prey on their own.

But not tonight.

The smoking ruins of the base were a charnel house. The

bodies of the slain littered the floors and hallways of the control building. Her cell didn't work. The base radio had been shot to bits. The question now was whether or not the attack had been noticed by anyone else. It didn't help that the base was in a remote area and had been abandoned for quite some time.

It's not exactly like the neighbors are going to hear the fight next door and dial 911, she thought.

The imperative was clear, though. She had to establish contact with the outside world. And soon. Because of her second problem.

Unsteadily, she rose from the desk. She swayed as she gained her feet and had to grip the edge of the desk to remain standing. She sucked breath to quell the dizziness that swam in her head and then made her way toward the door. Exiting the room, she made her way down the hall, holding onto the walls for support. Two doors down from the radio room was an ad-hoc sickbay Aripov's men had established for their own use. Its supplies were minimal – barely more than a few First Aid kits – but it had been enough for Sara to sterilize and bandage up her shoulder wound.

The problem was that she had to keep switching dressings because she was, slowly but surely, bleeding out. The bullet was still in there, but close to the surface of the skin. She could actually *feel* its hard edges whenever she swabbed the wound. Even a semi-skilled medic could likely remove it without difficulty! But for now, she was glad it was in there, exerting enough pressure to help stem the blood flow. Sepsis was less of a threat to her than literally bleeding to death.

She shrugged out of her jacket and then began the treacherous task of removing her shirt. Moving her bicep the wrong way caused waves of pain to roar from her gunshot wound to the very center of her solar plexus.

Pain keeps you awake, she remembered. And in her case, remaining awake meant staying alive. Because if she passed out here and now, the likelihood she would bleed out and die was quite high.

She managed to remove her shirt. Fingering another roll of bandages from the army First Aid kit, she began thinking her way through the next steps of dressing her wound. That's when the next wave of dizziness hit, and she began to crumple to the ground.

Jesus!

She arrested her fall by gripping the edge of the table and managed to slow her descent. But she was soon on her knees and wobbling. Moments later, the darkness swam into her head again and she was out like a light.

* * * * *

Just as Sara Durell was sinking into oblivion in Uzbekistan, Shakira was awaking in her bed in the village.

Another day, she thought and stretched. She sat up in bed and swiveled to put her feet to the floor.

As she did each morning, she reached for the wrapped bundle containing her running shoes. Running was becoming addictive to her, as her friend Washington had warned it would. His talk had contained all sorts of complicated English words for bodily chemicals, fluids which enhanced or inhibited athletic performance. He said she would come to rely on these for a mental and emotional boost. And she often felt that strange surge of joy within her once she overcame the initial body shock of exercise and fell into stride. But that wasn't the only reason she ran.

She thought of the American she had met at Tarak's camp and was filled with respect for his bravery. Coming halfway around the world to rescue his friends seemed to her an act worthy of the greatest admiration. That he would risk his life was at once inexplicable but also incredibly attractive to her.

Why do people do the hard things? she wondered. She supposed that was the way God had made human beings. Perhaps that urge to strive, to overcome obstacles and grow was part of His plan for Man...

All Shakira knew was that she enjoyed running and needed it as much as three meals per day or sleep.

She crept to the door of her aunt's house and let herself out. All around her, the village slumbered in the pre-dawn gloom. She stretched and began jogging down the narrow path between doorways to the edge of the desert.

Mafuz was piling up wood for that day's fire as she approached his hut. The blacksmith paused and straightened, waving her down.

"Good morning, blacksmith!" She jogged lightly in place, grinning at the old man.

"Good morning, little sister," he said kindly. But worry clouded his face. "Listen, Shakira, I think you should be very careful in your running this day. I was awakened some time ago by an explosion and the sound of gunfire coming from the direction of the base. You must stay away! I am very concerned you might be hurt or killed!"

The American, she thought.

It had to be him.

"Thank you, Mafuz," she said courteously. "I appreciate your warning and will heed your advice. Good day to you."

And she struck off in a different direction.

But once out of sight of the village, she switched course and made for the base.

She couldn't help herself.

CHAPTER 42

The silencer coughed and Tarak Khan's bullets sang toward their targets. At once, three of Amwar's bandits stiffened and dropped to the sand. Cody admired the man's marksmanship.

The remaining hoods let go the struggling woman and fumbled for their weapons. Cody rose, his right arm flashing up in a blur. Two loud reports sounded in quick succession, *blam-blam!* Two more fell, leaving a third, who turned and ran.

"I get him!" Tarak hurtled down the hill after him. That a desert bandit leader would so readily expose himself in battle surprised Cody. But then again, perhaps Khan had been after the guy for some time. He put the thought aside and descended the hill toward the partially-topless woman. She seemed to have recovered her wits and something of her dignity after the attempted gang rape. Still holding her slashed top over her breasts, she nevertheless knelt by the side of the unconscious male bicycler, tending to him. Cody skidded to a stop and knelt beside her as he felt for a pulse in the downed man.

"You okay?" he asked her. "Did they cut you? Break any bones?"

"No." The woman's accent was Scandinavian. An attractive blonde, she seemed fit and resilient. "But Sven here is…"

The man groaned and sat up, wincing and massaging his temples. He said something in their shared language and then he and the woman were chattering at each other. Cody had a mental stress flash of the Swedish Chef from the Muppets as they jabbered on, that cloth puppet making about as much sense as the two of them did.

"I'm sorry." The woman turned back. "We are the Bjornsons. I'm Magda and this is Sven. We're doing an extreme bicycle tour through the Near East…"

"You're aware you're in a warzone?" Cody managed to keep his voice under control, despite his rising annoyance. "A warzone in which American, British, Canadian and coalition forces shed their blood, lost their comrades and paid a huge price to keep the wolves from your door?"

Magda was nodding. "Yes, yes," she said. "Of course, of course. The narrative of western moral superiority. White privilege and power extending itself to all corners of the Earth. It sounds like you've really swallowed the whole 'white savior' narrative. But then again, I don't talk much about politics."

"Probably a good idea, because you obviously don't have the slightest idea what the hell you're talking about." Cody checked his watch. "You and your boyfriend there better mount up and peddle thataway." He pointed. "Because the shit's about to hit the fan around here."

"That language is obscene."

"Not as obscene as what's about to happen to the airbase on the other side of yonder rise. In another two hours, it's going to light up with a full-spectrum bombing strike courtesy of the United States Air Force. Everything within a mile will be obliterated. If you don't want to get killed, I suggest you mount your little bike toys and skedaddle right away."

Just then, Tarak Khan appeared, striding toward Cody and the Bjornsons. He shoved a man ahead of him, the one with the high-pitched giggle Cody had noted before. From the man's clumsy, disheveled appearance, it seemed Tarak might have roughed him up a bit before bringing him around.

"Jack Cody! This little *asshole...*" Tarak slapped the man sharply on the back of the head. "Is..." *Slap!* "Amwar. Amwar, kneel!"

The man half-turned to Khan, but the bandit leader replied by seizing a hank of Amwar's hair and dragging until his rival was on his knees.

"Now! Apologize to nice lady!"

Amwar, the rival bandit thief, was babbling incoherently. Obviously scared out of his wits, he was responding with the classic bully's reaction to being caught out – absolute terror. Aside from terrorizing tourists, Cody wondered what other sorts of nonsense he got up to.

Amwar spat.

Khan grabbed his hair, spun him around and smashed him across the mouth with the butt of the Walther. Amwar uttered a muffled scream of pain as his lips were raked and a few teeth displaced. Khan pressed the muzzle of the silencer against Amwar's left eye.

"Apologize!"

"I sorry!"

"Again!"

"I apolo…*GIIIIIIIZE!*"

Khan squeezed the trigger. The Walther coughed. And half the contents of Amwar's skull spilled out onto the sand. Sven groaned. Magda spun around and vomited on her shoes. And Amwar's body slumped the ground like a sack of rotten potatoes.

Cody turned to the Bjornsons.

"You guys better get out of here now."

They didn't say another word. The woman retrieved the first bike's wheel from behind a bush, affixed it and mounted. A second later, Sven mounted the other one. With a clicking of gears, they set out down the trail, back in the direction they had come.

Cody turned to Khan. "Looks like you've eliminated your major competition in one fell swoop."

"Competition?" Khan spat. "Amwar and his gang are shit. We leave their bodies here in the sand for the wild dogs. Allah can have mercy on his corpse. I will not."

"We probably don't have time for a funeral, anyway."

"Yes." Khan nodded. "Exactly."

His men had followed their lead and posted up nearby a short distance away. Cody stood at Khan's side as he delivered orders to his men in a clipped, urgent tone. With a gesture, they scattered to their tasks as Khan put a hand on Cody's shoulder and gestured with his head: *let's go.*

A short distance away was a hilltop. Dropping to his knees, Khan began climbing toward the summit. Cody fell in beside him. Thirty seconds later, they were peering over the brow of the hill.

"There," Khan whispered.

There it was – the operational target. Omega-1. For the first time since the mission began, Cody had a sense of the Marines he would be rescuing. Like he could sense them nearby. He would see them soon.

Soon.

CHAPTER 43

Khan sent scouts ahead of the MRAP to recon the base environs. They returned quickly with news.

"My scouts say all is clear. But Massoud has put a sentry out along the road. Man in chair with gun and phone."

"That's all you need, really."

"Jack Cody. If we take care of this man, our job will be that much easier."

"Well..." He checked his watch. "The clock is ticking. Let's go."

Khan led the way from the MRAP, which was parked at the foot of a hill. On the other side lay the base. Khan went upright for most of his circumnavigation of the hill but crouched as they came around to the far end. Cody saw the elevated berm of the paved road ahead, and the drainage ditch running alongside it. Two hundred yards further up, with his back to them, sat a man in a plastic lawn chair, swaddled in a cheap blanket. Cody knew from experience that the shank of the dog watch was toughest on anyone guarding a post. Something about the early hours of dawn made falling asleep almost irresistible.

They crept to the drainage ditch. It was sandy in the bottom, and quiet going. Khan had brought them to within one hundred yards of the guard when suddenly they heard a sound. It was a two-toned chime, not a desert sound but a piece of electronica. *Cellphone,* Cody realized. Khan froze when the guard moved, removing the phone from his pocket.

"*Salaam.*"

It must have been a man check, for there was no chatter from the guard's end. Just a lengthy silence during which he listened. Khan seized that opportunity to produce his Walther and silencer again. At length, the sentry ended the conversation and hung up. But to Cody's surprise, he did not huddle back into his blankets but instead rose and began moving to the edge of the road. They heard pants unzip and then the long, sizzling plash of the guy taking a leak onto gravel.

They waited.

And when the guard was done and walking back to his chair, Khan rose, aimed and put a bullet directly in the back of his skull. The man froze and tumbled forward, hitting the gravel by the roadside with a soft crunch. Then they were up out of the drainage ditch and approaching the body.

"Check his pockets," said Cody. "He may have keys."

Khan nodded and did as Cody bid. Cody, meanwhile, went to the chair and picked up the man's AK and cellphone. Having both might come in handy. He returned to Khan.

"Keys, Jack Cody." Khan held them aloft and shook them

before tossing them over. Cody caught and pocketed them.

"I've got his cellphone. And here's another rifle for your men." He handed it over. "The road to the base gate is clear."

Khan smiled thinly. "Time to attack," he said.

* * * * *

"Showalter. Ready?"

"Yes, LT."

"McKnight?"

"Ready, LT."

They were in the "ready-set" position by the gate enclosure that Watson had had them drill over and over again. Today was the day.

Breakout day.

From across the base, they could her the thin crunch of the approaching guard's footsteps. Everyone else would still be bedded down, the hour of morning prayer not yet upon them. But it was General Massoud's wish that the infidels be checked on in the pre-dawn hours. And so each morning, the slop bucket of the prisoners' breakfast was delivered in the wee hours by a lone guard who unlocked and entered their cage.

Every day he opens the shunt yard gate, Watson repeated to herself. *He crosses the yard. Twenty-two steps. Then he pulls out keys and unlocks the lock. There is a pause as he puts the lock in his belt pouch. Then he slides the chain free.*

The pause during which he stowed the lock.

That was what they were waiting for.

They heard the shunt yard gate open. Watson counted twenty-two steps. She held her breath as the lock was opened. She heard the chain clink as he lifted it free. Then his robes ruffling as he stowed it.

"NOW!" she whispered.

Showalter and McKnight hit the gate with their shoulders. The unjoined chain clattered loose as the gate burst wide. Then Watson was out, head down, going for the guard with a shoulder tackle.

She connected. It couldn't have been more perfect. The guard went down with a quiet *'oof!'* while his gun clattered off to the side, where McKnight snatched it up. Then Watson was clawing the guard's throat with her fingers. She found the larynx and latched onto it. Gripped, lifted and twisted. *Pop!* It shot loose, quivering in her fingers like a baby octopus dropping red as the final pulses of the guard's dying breath seeped from it.

Watson looked up.

Silence.

And the shunt-yard gate stood wide.

She rose. "Come on," she whispered.

And she led them.

* * * * *

In the hills close by the base, a lone girl ran through the pre-dawn dark.

Shakira knew what was about to happen. She understood that what her man Tarak and the American were doing was unbelievably dangerous. The likelihood they would survive was by no means assured. She doubted there were many places in Afghanistan more dangerous than the old French base right now.

And yet she had to be here.

They had come too far, risked too much and lost everything. The Afghan people – the rural villagers, the nomads, the poor and destitute – had endured half a century of oppression. First the Russian tanks, then the whip of the Taliban. When the Americans had come for their brief sojourn here in this land of a thousand suns, a brief glimpse of another possible future had emerged. Yes, the Americans had gone home. But they had left behind something no previous invader had.

Relationships.

None of the Taliban, nor the Soviets, nor the Imperialist British had ever done for the people what Washington had done for her, what the French had done for Mafuz and what Jack Cody was doing now for his friends. They had taken the risk and dared the friendship of strangers, offering a part of themselves for...

What?

And that was what made her run. It had nothing to do with gaining and everything to do with giving. If the day ever came when they needed her, she would run to the ends of the Earth for her village. When the people had needed the Americans, they had come. Just as the great Prophet had come from *Allah* and given the Word to Mankind.

Power was not about taking but about giving. And the

greatest form of giving was that of personal sacrifice.

So she ran.

And suddenly, the dark sky above was filled with a blaze of flame and the roar of explosions. The day of liberation had arrived.

CHAPTER 44

Tarak, sitting behind the wheel of the MRAP, turned and thumped twice on the wall separating the cab from the rear compartment. When he received two thumps in return, he glanced out the windshield at the road ahead. A low rise separated them from the base gate.

"We are ready, Jack Cody," he said.

Cody produced the remote detonator. During his last recon of the base, he had detonated a suite of the shaped charges he'd placed on various pieces of equipment. But more charges remained – many more. He flicked the switch that activated the remote detonator and prepped it for action.

"Stay tuned for rockets' red glare," he said quietly. And threw the switch.

Somewhere on the base, a piece of military hardware detonated in a roar of flame. From their vantage on the road, they could see the light from the explosion, feel the ground shake and actually see bits of debris scatter. But then Khan had started the vehicle, thrown on the high beams and was barreling down the road toward the fence.

BA-BOOM! A second explosion split the night. They topped the rise and began hurtling toward the guard post at the main entrance. Cody racked the bolt of the C8, leaned out the passenger side window and fired a burst that scattered the sentries manning the gate as another tank went up in flames.

Tarak Khan leaned forward in his seat, both hands gripping the wheel, his right leg extended to its full length pushing the accelerator to the floor. The gate rose in front of them. Khan let out some sort of battle cry in his native language the moment before the nose struck. The gate resisted briefly before bowing inward and blasting apart, its chains flying as the MRAP flew into the compound and screeched to a halt.

Cody bailed out the passenger side just as the rear doors opened and Tarak Khan's merry band of bloodthirsty bandits burst out, weapons blazing. As Cody watched, one of them knelt and fired a pistol at the back of a retreating guard. Massoud's man was caught mid-step, flung up onto his toes and then driven facedown by the force of the bullet.

Then the base began coming to life. The doorway of a nearby building burst open, and a handful of armed men tumbled out. The man with the flamethrower leveled his weapon on the group and squeezed off. A spray of liquid fire leapt from the hose in his hand, dousing the responding gunmen in a cloud of fire. They fell screaming, their robes in flames, the building from which they had come now wreathed in smoke and fire.

BA-BOOM! The next series of explosions began. It was a

row of trucks by the eastern fence of the base. Cody watched them go up one after another like fireworks. He heard screams and running footsteps as Massoud's men scrambled to react. While they did seem to have a plan for responding to an attack, their damage control game was lacking. Cody doubted they had bothered to bring any firefighting equipment along when establishing the base.

Khan skidded to a stop beside him.

"My men are attacking the main dormitory now!" he cried. "Jack Cody, we caught most of them asleep! I have a hundred pinned down in that building there!"

"Where's your flamethrower operator?"

Khan grinned. "He is on his way there, Jack Cody. We are about to have – how do you say? A barbecue!"

No sooner had Khan spoken than the stream of liquid fire burst forth again. It touched one corner of a two-storey wooden structure. The desert's head and aridity had combined to turn the building's structure into a perfect batch of kindling. It went up like a torch in the night.

"Look," whispered Khan, putting his hand to Cody's shoulder.

Cody looked. In between explosions and screams, the light of the combined fires illumined the façade of the wooden structure. As they watched, men began crowding toward the edge of the roof to avoid the flame. One stepped to the edge and then over…

Cody remembered the photographs of 9/11 in New York, the horrific sight of the "Falling Man" hurtling down from the wreckage of the World Trade Center towers. Now he watched his own succession of falling men, some burning, as they plunged to their deaths on the concrete below.

"They are confused. They are wounded. They are dying." Khan jerked his chin. "Now is time for you to rescue your friends, no?"

"Now is the time, yes."

Khan put out his hand. "Good luck, Jack Cody," he said.

"See you on the other side," he said. He shook Khan's hand and then began sprinting for the prisoners' enclosure.

All around him, the base burned.

Cody found himself thinking about the words of *The Star-Spangled Banner*. America's anthem recounted a battle during the War of 1812, one in which America's freedom was protected through blood and fire.

It's no different now, he thought. Freedom was never easy. It always had to be fought for.

It was his last thought as he rushed forward into a galaxy of darkness and flame.

CHAPTER 45

Watson, McKnight and Showalter spilled out of the shunt-yard onto the concrete apron of the base airfield just as the first explosions detonated. As one, they hit the ground.

"What the hell was that?" cried McKnight between blasts.

Watson listened, counting explosions, noting rhythm, tempo and variations in volume and length.

"Someone's attacking these bastards!" she cried.

"Who?" asked Showalter.

"Maybe Taliban?"

"Could be anyone! Doesn't matter!" Watson rolled to her knees and pointed. "Somewhere in that row of choppers is an Apache with our name on it! Let's go!"

They came again to their feet. Everywhere on the base was pandemonium. Shouts of panic rang in the air and Watson could see the distant forms of enemy soldiers dashing from buildings in search of the enemy. A whooshing sound in the middle distance caught her attention.

"Look!" she cried, pointing.

A stream of flame streaked out and engulfed a building near the main gate. Men screamed as flames tangled their robes and turned clothing into crematoriums.

"Somebody brought a flame-thrower to the party!" McKnight whooped.

"My kind of party," said Watson. She scanned the row of choppers ahead. "Nearly there! C'mon!"

All I've got to do is get in one of those birds and hot it up, she thought. Even if she couldn't take off, an activated Apache would bring a suite of weapons under her control that would do just as much damage as those shaped charges she heard going off (for that's what she had surmised they were). She fully intended to escape. But if that proved impossible, she planned to send as many of these bastards to hell as she possibly could before she died.

She skidded to a stop beside one chopper. McKnight and Showalter covered her as she ducked inside. She pushed through the main cabin to the cockpit and her heart sank.

Someone had been in here and stripped the cockpit of equipment. There were empty sockets and ports visible where an enemy mechanic had disconnected and removed controls. That they would have that sophisticated an airfield crew surprised her. But she filed the info away.

"It's been stripped," she said, dropping to the ground beside McKnight. "Controls removed. She can't fly."

"How about this one, LT?" Showalter pointed.

"Nnnnn... o." Watson squinted. "See the weapons racks?

Empty. And I'm betting the rounds have been removed from the chain gun. Looks like our friends have been scrounging for parts." She cast around. "Now...*there.*"

She pointed. A few hundred yards away, one Apache gleamed in the lights from the explosions. Bright, shiny, new – Watson recognized a fresh unit when she saw one. The Talis would have captured that one when they took an airfield. It even had inspection tags still clipped to the outside.

"C'mon." She touched Showalter's shoulder and led her men forward.

* * * * *

Abdul Massoud was jolted awake in his bunk by the force of the explosions. He awakened, disoriented as the last fragments of a dream tangled his mind. He shook his head, sat up and brought his feet to the floor.

"Report!" he bellowed.

At once, the door to his bedroom opened. He had set up quarters in one of the base office buildings, with a sentry at the door. The sentry was trembling and very obviously terrified.

"Great one! We are under attack!"

"Bring Gul here!" Massoud stood upright, stuffed his feet into sandals and reached for his sword.

Moments later, Gul appeared in the doorway.

"Great one, I –"

"What is going on?"

"We are not sure, Great one! Only that we are under attack!"

Gul, though confused, had at least pulled it together sufficiently to offer a coherent report. "We see no aircraft, yet there are explosions among the tanks and equipment! The gate has been breached by an American vehicle, yet the men we are fighting appear to be desert men like ourselves!"

Massoud's fury was volcanic. "Mercenaries? Bandits? Those NRF dogs?"

"We have no way of knowing, Great one!"

"*Then what good are you?*" Massoud's arm whipped back, the naked blade of his scimitar aimed at Gul's head. But at the last second, he restrained himself. Killing Gul would serve no purpose other than to satisfy his momentary anger. He needed his subaltern to help coordinate the defense.

"Go and gather what men you can and muster them here at once!" he cried. "We will marshal our forces and retake the base!"

"Yes, Great one!"

Gul wheeled and sprinted from the room. Massoud followed at a more sedate pace, the sentry falling in behind him as he moved to the front room of the office building with its windows that gave off onto the airfield itself.

Explosions rumbled the floor. Massoud could see the hot orange streamers of detonating charges blasting into the black sky and could hear the rattle of small-arms fire and men's shouts.

Under attack? Here? *Now?*

How is this possible?

Now his men were running toward the building. Massoud

counted a dozen, urged on by Gul. Massoud moved to the doorway and raised his blade. The men, recognizing it, clustered around him.

"Gul! Report!"

"The damage is terrible, Great one!" Gul flung a hand toward the latest explosion. "Rows of tanks and helicopters have been destroyed! The main gate is breached, and an armed vehicle is wreaking havoc on our men!"

"How many are the enemy?"

"No more than a dozen or two at most, Great one."

Massoud nodded. He turned to his men.

"We will divide into groups. You, you and you." He pointed. "Make for the gate and retake it. You men." He waved toward another pod of fighters. "Secure the jets by the east fence. The rest of you, follow me."

The group broke into its sections which scattered toward their assigned tasks.

CHAPTER 46

Cody could see the silhouettes of helicopters off to his left. Every now and then an explosion would go off, providing glimpses of the paint and markings on the choppers' sides. Cody remembered the shunt yard was not far from the rows of choppers. He paused, seeking for the generator station to orient himself.

There. He could see the low tin structure with the light not too far off. He switched direction and made for it. The generator was one of those charges he had not yet detonated. Cody wished he could claim it was foresight on his part, but it seemed to be just the random luck of the draw. *I'll take luck any day,* he thought.

He heard a cluster of voices talking in Pashtu and the sound of approaching footsteps. Cody dropped and rolled under a nearby truck. Just in time, as it happened. A moment later, a half-dozen pairs of sandaled feet appeared where he had stood. One man, obviously in command, was speaking, relaying orders to the others. As Cody watched, the group scattered.

He counted to ten and then rolled out from under the truck.

No sign of them.

The tin hut with the light outside that housed the generator was just ahead. Cody crouched low, moving fast between the vehicles until he was close enough to gain his bearings. He craned up, casting about for the prisoner enclosure when a sudden movement caused him to duck again.

Damn!

One of the men from the group had been sent to guard the generator. Cody had seen the man and ducked just as he was in the act of turning Cody's direction. There was absolutely no way to get to the prisoner enclosure without dealing with this guy first. Just detonating the place would rob Cody of the light necessary to make his way to the enclosure. So he hadn't much choice.

No two ways about it. The guard's end would have to be swift and silent.

Cody drew his knife and began circling around toward the back of the tin hut. The din of battle raging all around drowned out the sound of his footsteps. He reached the rear wall of the hut without incident and edged around the corner. No sign of anyone there, either. He crept along the wall until he could peer around to the open side of the enclosure.

The guard stood, an AK dangling from its strap. In absence of a sling, the guard had slung the assault rifle around his neck and one arm and was cradling the thing at gut level, both hands on the weapon. Cody would have preferred a guard who was indolent and lazy. But he supposed the threat of imminent death was enough to make even the most casual soldier snap to and raise his head. Cody waited until the man had his back turned before moving in, the dagger in his right fist, the other hand raised to grab.

Massoud's sentry chose that moment to turn. His eyes bugged wide when he saw Cody and he pivoted to bring the AK to bear. But two quick steps closed the gap until the distance between them was two narrow and then Cody's left hand was coming up.

"Aaaaaa-*mgrph*," he managed before Cody's hand covered his mouth.

The guard struggled to pull away, the AK swinging. The guard's hand dropped from the handle and gripped the stock. He swung, smashing Cody's left arm, causing him to drop his hand. The moment this happened, the guard opened his mouth and screamed.

Cody pounced, grasped the man's tunic and pushed. They tangled and crashed to the ground together. Cody pulled away, raised the knife and brought it down. The man squirmed, jerking to the right. The blade came down and entered his shoulder.

The man's scream coincided with another explosion. Cody reared back, seized the knife in both hands and brought it down. It sank into the man's chest. Cody withdrew and plunged it down, again and again. Within moments, the guard lay still.

Shakily, Cody gained his feet just as he saw three silhouettes charging toward him.

$$* * * * *$$

"There!" Watson cried, pointing.

McKnight and Showalter skidded to a stop, following her finger. The row of new choppers was just ahead. They switched direction and had taken two steps when a shadowy figure approached.

McKnight raised the AK.

"Wait!" Watson waved her arm. "Hold your fire!"

The shadow moving toward them was not a Tali. She could tell that much even from a distance. Something about the way he moved. Could it be...?

"Don't shoot!" the figure cried, raising his hands.

English? Watson frowned. Gesturing for McKnight to keep the man covered, she approached.

"Who the hell are you?" she demanded.

The man smiled and dropped his arms. "Name's Jack Cody," he said with a smile. "President Harwood sends his regards."

"Holy shit," whispered Showalter. "Is this a rescue?"

"It's a raid," said Cody. "Some of our local allies have decided enough is enough and threw in with us as a chance to rid the area of Abdul Massoud."

"Americans. Friendly Afghans. I don't give a crap," said Watson. "It's good to see you. Lieutenant Watson, United States Marine Corps. These two men are under my command. And we're getting the hell out of here."

"Got a plan?"

"Sure do." Watson pointed. "These helos are fresh off the assembly line. If I can get into one, I can hot it up and fly us out of here."

"Sounds good," said Cody. "Mind if I hitch a ride?"

"My pleasure, Mr. Cody." For the first time in days, Watson found her smile. "You guys cover me while I get this hatch open."

Cody, Showalter and McKnight fanned out, weapons raised as Watson fell to the Apache. The hatch itself was unlocked. But the damn thing was held in place by a zip-tie that just wouldn't let go.

"Cody? Got a knife?" she asked.

Cody opened his mouth to answer when the night was shattered by weapons fire.

CHAPTER 47

Onboard the USS *Ronald Reagan*, Captain Elijah Browne awoke in his bunk and pushed himself up on one elbow. All around him droned the comforting, familiar sounds of a carrier underway. The sounds had a soothing, narcotizing effect on him most of the time. But Browne's awareness was peaking at high-trigger alert. His mind was rimmed with the simmering red edge that came with knowing the time had come. It was zero hour.

Time to hit the line.

He rolled from his rack, stocking feet hitting the floor. He stepped into his flight suit and zipped up. His helmet and other equipment waited in the locked bay by the pilots' ready room. Stuffing his feet into boots, he took time to check his comms. There had been no adjustment to the mission clock, no change in orders. They were still going in. And they were going in now.

He emerged from his cabin and followed the companion-way to the stairs that would bring him to the ready room. The ship's corridors and stairwells were quiet at this hour. His pilots would already be mustering up for their final pre-flight briefing. Expecting to meet no one on the way, he was surprised by the sight of the ship's captain waiting in the corridor outside the ready room.

"Captain Browne," he said quietly. "Just wanted to confirm in person that we've had no change in orders. And to wish you luck."

"Thank you, sir." Browne came to attention. The captain nodded and disappeared through a hatch. Browne's hand fell to the handle of the ready room door.

His pilots came to their feet, each attired in his flight suit. Browne went to the head of the room and stood behind the desk.

"Be seated," he said, and waited until his men were before continuing. "We're going in. Our orders stand. No change in operational planning. But there has been a development you need to know about.

"At our last briefing, I informed you all about Operation REDEMPTION, the Delta Force op to infiltrate Omega-1 and rescue American personnel being held prisoner by General Massoud's forces. Delta Force helos went in and encountered unexpected resistance. We all know Army Delta's reputation as solid operators. Unfortunately, despite their planning and expertise, their progress was stalled by unforeseen forces. The Delta team became pinned down by enemy aircraft. Despite their efforts to resist, they were overwhelmed. According to our reports, the entire team was compromised."

One pilot raised his hand. "Sir, have they been captured?"

"Negative." Browne hesitated for just the barest second. "The entire team was killed."

A shocked silence settled over the group.

"They carried the fight to the enemy. And they lost. We will mourn them when there is time. But for now... Our business is in-country, and our orders are clear. There will be no scrubbing the mission. The objective is clear. We're on the clock. And we're up."

As one, the pilots remained expressionless as this news settled.

"Pre-flight and weapons check status?"

"Complete, sir," confirmed his second-in-command quietly.

"Alright then." Browne nodded. "Suit up. Good luck. And good hunting."

The pilots piled into the locker bay, grabbing up their helmets and gear from the racks. Browne tucked his helmet under his arm and watched as his men fitted their headgear and oxygen masks into place and check one another's gear. Once he was satisfied they were done, he turned and led the way up to the flight deck where the crew chief awaited.

"Birds are set, sir," said the chief. "All pre-flight checks complete, weapons hot."

"That's what I like to hear."

"Good luck, sir."

Browne's pilots moved quickly to their assigned aircraft, each attended by a flight crew member that stood by as the pilots did a walk-around and undercarriage check. Then they held the ladder for each man as he climbed to the cockpit and then removed it as the cockpit bubble closed.

Darkness hovered over the Indian Ocean. The black outlines of the F-35s were sharp against the halogen glare of the deck lights. Despite his many years in aviation, a part of Browne still churned in excitement at the merest glimpse of an operational combat aircraft. The boy he was would have been thrilled at the sight of these cutting-edge weapons lined up and ready for action.

The stars were still visible, but already their sharpness was beginning to fade as the black of night bled out. Browne knew the signs of impending dawn. He checked his watch.

They were right on schedule.

Browne's jet was the closest. The crew chief stood by as he finished his walkaround, fitted his helmet and mask in place and then began clambering up the ladder. One big step and he was over the side, settling into his cockpit seat. With the touch of a button, the cockpit bubble lowered, settling into place and sealing with a pressurized hiss. Browne engaged his engines. As the steady whine rose in his ears, he dropped his finger to the switch activating his mission read-out screen.

You never know, he thought. *A sudden change of plans. A last minute reprieve. It could happen…*

But no. There was no such message.

It was time.

The orange glare of the deck chief's glow sticks shimmered in the gloom ahead. They twirled with a 'come on' motion. Browne touched the controls to begin taxiing forward. When the glowsticks crossed into an X formation he stopped, steered and pivoted the nose of the jet onto the carrier's apron.

The runway stretched ahead, dotted either side with running lights. Browne settled his ship into take-off position, waiting until the deck trap was raised behind him to catch the back-blast of the engines. Browne made an instrument adjustment and the turbines howled, rising in pitch toward the scream they would become just before take-off.

Ahead glimmered the Indian Ocean and the empty sky that would lead to their target.

Browne waited until the engines' shrill was at maximum din then punched the throttle. The carrier's runway ripped past below his wheels.

Then he was airborne.

CHAPTER 48

"Damn it!"

Cody gritted his teeth and squinted into the gloom. The group of Massoud's men – the same from which he'd first hidden by rolling under the truck – had circled back. *Probably heard the guard scream,* he thought. And now here they were, weapons ablaze. Soon they would attract others.

They were pinned down near the chopper Watson had been struggling to access. So far as Cody could tell by the flash-glare from the next explosion, the enemy numbered about a dozen. His C8 and the AKs in the hands of the two Marines were holding them off. For now. Cody glanced at Watson, dropped a hand to his holster and drew the Beretta.

"Here." He offered it to her, handle first.

Watson accepted the pistol smoothly, checked the action and then glanced back at the chopper.

"If I can get in there, this game will change," she vowed. "You got that knife?"

Cody nodded. "Let's clear that front rank, first."

"Sounds good."

He watched her take her stance, raise the pistol in the classic two-handed marksman's grip and fire. Two men went down and the three beside them scattered, chased by bullets. Watson spent her rounds wisely and shot true. *Definitely a keeper,* thought Cody.

"LT!" One of the Marines, the man she'd called McKnight, was pointing.

Another group of Massoud's goons was rushing to reinforce the one that had engaged them. If that trend continued, they were finished. What was needed was a game-changer. Cody cleared away nearby stragglers with a burst of fire, then drew his dagger.

"Here," he said, handing it to Watson. "I'm going to provide a distraction. Once that happens, you should have time to cut that strap and get inside."

"Roger that." She accepted the blade. "What sort of distraction."

"This kind." He drew a fragmentation grenade from his belt.

"The best kind," she said with a grin.

Cody pulled the pin and hurled the weapon straight into the front rank of the advancing enemy. It detonated in a sheet of orange fire, the shockwave of the explosion blasting apart the beds of two transport trucks parked nearby. A half-dozen of the enemy were cut down. And by then, Watson was doing some cutting of her own.

"Got it!" The zip-tie parted, and the hatch rolled open. Cody retreated to the edge of the chopper, providing covering fire for the other two Marines to gain the hatch and scramble inside. Cody fired off one last burst from the C8 before turning to see what Watson had in mind.

She had gained the cockpit. Her hands floated over the control panel. But instead of engaging the rotors, Cody heard the whine of the sixty-cal chain-gun spinning up and being brought to bear.

"FIRE IN THE HOLE!" she screamed. And the world was filled with the deafening blast of weapons fire.

* * * * *

"Great one!" Gul stumbled into the second-floor room of the base office building from which Massoud was directing his men. "The prisoners have escaped and armed themselves!"

Massoud brought his fist down on the window ledge. All his work of the past days, sending his men to scout for, reclaim and transport abandoned American weapons and vehicles to this site was proving to be for naught. And now the very men and woman who had been his prize were loose and hell-bent on re-venge. Normally, he dealt with mistakes by imposing the death penalty on offenders. But this was easiest when the offenders in question were his own loyal followers. Armed enemy soldiers were another matter.

An explosion – this one smaller – blossomed in the area where the new helicopters had been positioned.

"Grenade," Massoud said aloud. That had to be where the

enemy was positioned. That or somewhere very nearby.

He turned and moved from the window, steps heavy with purpose. Brushing past Gul, he moved through the doorway and descended the stairs. A hush fell among his men as he appeared in the main room downstairs. All watched him with the intense, patient expectancy followers of The Way had of behaving in his presence. There was no God but God, but the Great One had the power and influence of at least a minor prophet.

"All our work!" Massoud drew his scimitar and brandished it. "Our victories for Islam! All these things now risk being stolen from us!"

The assembled men nodded mutely, stroking their weapons, awaiting the Great One's orders.

Massoud inhaled deeply, fighting the panic that rose within. He had to seem assured. Powerful. Unafraid. Even as his treasures detonated and his reputation among the terrorist leaders assembled here for the auction plummeted.

"I want them taken alive!" he thundered. "The Americans we captured have escaped and are doing this! *All* this! They must never have the chance to escape again! *And they must pay!*"

As one, the men muttered their assent, even as the dull crump of explosions reverberated outside.

"You will assemble and follow me!" Massoud continued, pointing with his sword. "We will capture them alive! And we will allow them to follow in the footsteps of their hero and savior!"

The assembled men held their breath and waited.

"Gul! Gather wood! Hammer and nails! I want you to take three men and build crosses! Big ones! Strong and heavy enough to support the weight of one man each! We will recapture these infidel killers and crucify them outside the gate for all to see!"

One might have expected a cheer or some other demonstration of approval. But this was Abdul Massoud and these were followers of The Way. His suggestion was met by mute obedience. And when he raised his sword and led the way to battle, they followed meekly.

CHAPTER 49

Ten miles out from the Pakistani coastline, Captain Elijah Browne and his squadron dropped to two thousand feet. The F-35s swung into a tight formation to present as small a radar target as possible. On Browne's orders, they were set to activate afterburners and accelerate to Mach 1 for their transit across Pakistani airspace.

Browne made final adjustments to his own bird. He felt absolutely no remorse whatsoever about breaching a sovereign nation's airspace. He had been privileged to personally meet President Obama during his last year in office. Browne, a man of few heroes, held that President in particular esteem. President Obama had personally made the decision not to warn Pakistan about the SEAL raid that killed bin Laden. Browne and his crew would be moving too fast and be in country too short a time to do any comparable damage. But transit Pakistani airspace they would, with or without the host government's permission. If it was okay for President Obama to make that call and the Navy SEALs to go in, then he felt it was okay for he and his men to do likewise.

Besides, they had a job to do.

"All aircraft, this is combat flight leader. We are t-minus 30 seconds to Mach 1 on my mark... Mark."

He started the clock on his control panel. Eight seconds into the count, his picket squawked through with a priority call.

"Combat flight leader, this is Raptor 2. I have aircraft inbound. Transponder signals confirm: Pakistani air force."

"What is their status?"

"Sir, confidence is high. I – wait... Correction! Correction! They're painting us! Repeat! *They are painting us!*"

Browne's jaw firmed. That meant the Pakistani pilots were locking weapons on his team. His fist slammed the transmit switch of his mic.

"All birds, delay jump to Mach 1! Raptor 3, Raptor 4... break from formation! Engage enemy and bring to ground!"

With a roaring whoosh, Raptor 3 and 4 broke from formation and streaked out toward the Pakistani jets. The enemy birds were Dassault Mirage aircraft, effective attack air platforms but hardly state of the art. Accounting for all differences in speed, maneuverability and armament, pitting a Mirage against an F-35 was like attacking an aircraft carrier in a rubber dinghy.

The Pakistani pilot's voice rippled in Browne's headset:

"American aircraft! Turn back from our airspace or we will open –"

The message died in a spray of static. His men were initiating standard combat assault procedures, beginning with signal jamming the enemy's comms. The Mirages reacted immediately, each peeling off in its own direction. Raptor 3 and 4 split to follow them. Browne wondered which of the two would be first to down a Mirage. He didn't have to wait long to find out.

Raptor 3's Mirage began a steep climb in a vain hope of outpacing the F-35. But within moments, 3 was upon him, target painted and locked. An AIM-120 AMRAAM missile streaked out from its weapons bay in a plume of afterburn. An instant later, the Mirage vaporized. Literally blown to bits, it fell in a spray of shrapnel toward the Indian Ocean.

Raptor 4's kill took a while longer. The second Pakistani pilot was not only desperate to survive – he was also quite good. Knew all the tricks. He did the Wild Weasel, the Crazy Ivan, the Duck and Roll. But in the end, Raptor 4 closed the gap and shot him at point-blank range. Browne's pilot ended up skating his F-35 through a blast cloud of debris, then slaloming around to rejoin formation.

Once both pilots had closed up ranks, a cheer arose across the radio channel. Each pilot in the squadron was exalting at the kills, at their combined success. They were Browne's Bastards. Their morale was high. And they had just added two more kills to their squadron tally. Browne let the cheer go on for exactly thirty seconds before cutting it off.

"This is combat flight leader. All birds, prep for jump to Mach 1 in 10 seconds on my mark. Mark."

The radio channel fell silent. Browne's preparations were already made. He watched his dash clock spin down to zero.

Then he hit his afterburners.

His plane leapt forward like a horse with its tail on fire. His men were right with him, burn for burn. The entire combat group became a blurry black arrow in the skies above Pakistan, hurtling along at the speed of sound, ringing sonic booms across the sky like the bells of doom. On his tracking screen, Browne noted a few futile efforts to track or paint his men. But no sooner had the F-35s appeared than they were gone.

Ghost riders in the sky, thought Browne.

Pakistan came. Pakistan went. As they approached the border with Afghanistan, Browne ordered the group to their bombing ceiling.

As one, they climbed. Up the long, delirious burning blue, just like the poem. Browne had never lost his fundamental wonder at aircraft, aviation and the fundamental miracle of defying gravity. That mankind should achieve such a feat and turn it to war struck him as no surprise.

It's always been about the high ground, he thought. *From Gettysburg to Baghdad.* War never changed. Browne lived with that by joining wonder to reason. He flew to kill other men. But...

He flew.

They leveled out at 8,000 feet. The dark aircraft spread apart, glimmering like a colony of titanium bats in the above-cloud sunlight. They were now too high and moving too fast to be endangered by any other aircraft. But they were no longer at Mach 1. The afterburners chewed up too much gas at that speed. They had to keep some in the tank for the cruise back to the *Reagan*.

Browne touched his transmit switch:

"All birds, this is combat flight leader. Assume cruising formation and begin pre-bombing cross-checks. Stand by for heads up."

Browne clicked off and checked his dashboard clock.

They had been airborne for seven minutes and were now fifteen minutes out from target.

For God and country, he thought. And began his cross-checks.

CHAPTER 50

Watson leaned on the fire control switch of the chain gun. The weapon bucked and chattered in its swivel housing, fanning back and forth into the row of charging Talis. Fragging them.

Cody watched, crouched in the chopper's rear beside Showalter and McKnight. Watson was going at it with a vengeance, days of pent-up rage pouring out in waves of smooth, ruthless, deadly force. Cody knew battle fever when he saw it, and Watson's had a temperature of 103.

Showalter tapped his shoulder and pointed.

Vehicles were approaching their position from the south. Cody counted six. Whoever was leading them was cautious: the lead vehicle was careful to remain behind two rows of tanks as it approached their position. *This will be the main body,* Cody thought. Coming in force.

Watson, meanwhile, was mopping up the first wave. Those left were scattered and disorganized, retreating through the rows of equipment at a staggering stumble. They were broken and would not be back. But the second force was massing.

At length, the chain gun fell silent. Cody stepped forward into the cockpit and dropped his hand to Watson's shoulder.

"We've got company," he told her. "Behind us. About two rows back. A lot of them."

"Okay." Watson's hands fell to the flight stick. "If you can buy me five minutes, I can get us airborne." She looked up and began her pre-flight check.

"We'll do what we can."

Cody turned back toe the rear compartment. Showalter was still there but poised by the hatch. McKnight had stepped out but still had one foot inside the chopper.

"They're coming in fast," he said. "Be here in less than a minute."

Cody craned his neck and squinted at the sky. "How long until sunrise?"

McKnight shrugged. "Ten. Fifteen minutes."

"That's all we have to hold them off for. Watson can get us airborne in five. And if she can't, we'll be removed courtesy of the United States Air Force?"

"Rescue mission?" Showalter asked hopefully.

Cody shook his head. "Saturation bombing run. This whole base will be blown right back into the Stone Age."

"Oh." Showalter's face fell.

"I say we go kill a bunch of these assholes," McKnight said. He shrugged again. "Can't hurt either way."

Cody grinned. He liked this guy.

They deployed out from the chopper, moving forward at a crouch so as not to expose their positions. The chopper itself was made obvious by the bullet holes in its fuselage and smoke rising from its recently discharged guns. Now its rotor was beginning to turn, slowly and gently at first until gaining speed. The engine began its slow climb to a whine; it would take time for the chopper to spin up.

The trucks were closing in. Cody, Showalter and McKnight were staged up, concealed among the shanks and shadows of a row of tanks. From their concealed position they would be able to furnish Watson with plenty of cover.

The line of vehicles was closing in. Cody counted: *eight*. Eight SUVs packed with Massoud's troops. One minute gone and four more to go. They just had to hold for four more minutes...

In the moment between the vehicles' coming to a stop and their doors opening, Cody sprang upright and sprayed them with weapon's fire. The four or so doors which had begun to edge open slammed closed. Glass windows caved on the vehicles not equipped with armored glass. Tires exploded and hissed flat. In the silence as Cody swapped magazines, he heard voices calling out commands in Pashtu. Some of the commanders that had managed to hold it together were mustering their troops on the other side, preparing a counterattack. Meanwhile, the pitch of the chopper's engine climbed.

Cody glanced back at it ...

Two minutes gone, now. They need only hold three more.

A chatter of automatic fire rose from behind the vehicles. Rounds buzzed and struck, spraying off the armor of the tanks behind which the three Americans sheltered. Cody was thankful they had three rows of vehicles between themselves and the enemy. It was too far for accurate shots at the chopper, and way too far for a grenade to be hurled. But he was sure that was coming.

He switched the C-8 to semi-auto and sighted through the scope. Near as he could make out, the line of enemy shooters was armed almost exclusively with small-arms – pistols and AKs. One sighted along a sniper's rifle toward the whirling rotors of Watson's chopper. Cody didn't like the sight of that.

Drawing a breath, exhaling, half-drawing and then holding it in, he steadied the sights on the sniper's forehead and fired.

Bullseye. The man tumbled.

Three minutes gone. He glanced back at the whirling rotor blades, squinted against the roaring engine. *Almost there...*

He bent back to the scope.

The number of Talis returning fire had diminished. Cody was sure some had been dropped, but not this many. Which could only mean one thing.

They're flanking us.

He ceased fire and drew back, holding up a fist. Showalter and McKnight followed suit, ceasing engagement.

Cody gestured toward his eyes with two fingers: *watch.* Then he swept a hand in a wide semi-circle toward the enemy position. His two Marines got the idea. They split the line into three and began scanning. It took Showalter less than a minute to see it.

He whistled loud and hard, pointing.

Cody squinted.

Stinger!

The orange at the wedding.

And it was coming this way.

They retreated full tilt. Showalter got there first, grabbed Watson by the shoulder and hauled at her.

"LT! Stinger!"

That was all she needed to hear. Watson bailed from the pilot's chair. She leapt from the hatch and fell in beside Cody and McKnight. They ran as far and as fast as they could before throwing themselves to the ground as the Stinger roared and the Apache went up in a ball of flame and shrapnel.

CHAPTER 51

Browne's attack squadron roared across the border into Afghanistan at bombing altitude. If their presence was noted by Afghan air traffic control, Browne saw no indication.

They could scramble fighters, he thought. *No reason why not.* But there was nothing in the Taliban's arsenal capable of climbing to their altitude in a timely enough manner to stop the bombing run. And nothing quick or strong enough to chase and shoot them down before they turned for home. From the perspective of enemy countermeasures, they were as safe as could be for now.

He hit the transmit switch and addressed his pilots:

"Raptor 2, Raptor 5. Stage out for pre-bombing recon run. Raptor 3,4 and 6. Initiate targeting sequence. Set navigation protocols. We're in the chute."

He watched as Raptors 2 and 5 broke from formation, both F-35 kicking on their afterburners and accelerating to half-Mach for their recon pass over the target. They would make a low pass to check for other aircraft or missile batteries before sweeping back to rejoin the squadron.

Browne wasn't overly concerned about encountering resistance at this point. Even assuming the Talis had managed to put their hands to American aircraft capable of opposing his team, he doubted very much they had pilots with the skill or the stomach to do so. But standard procedures were just that: standard. He would take every precaution before leading his birds into battle.

Meanwhile, visible through wisps of broken clouds, the land below passed – a crust of brown broken here and there by strewn rubble and blasted cities. Browne had done one tour in country and inflicted more than his fair share of damage on the place. For him, Afghanistan was far off and way down there. But he was under no illusion about the everyday lives that transpired below.

"Combat flight leader, this is Raptor 5."

Browne punched his transmit button. "Go, Raptor 5."

"Initial recon sortie complete. No resistance. No planes, we were never painted or fired on by rockets."

"That's good news, Raptor 5."

"Some indications of fighting underway, sir. Thermal imaging read explosions and possible concussion from weapons fire."

That would be their CIA unit in country, he thought. *Raisin' hell.*

No reason he and his men couldn't support that effort.

"All birds, this is flight leader. Cut air speed by twenty knots and proceed to target."

Browne clicked off.

By reducing speed, his squadron's arrival would be delayed. No doubt the operatives on the ground were aware of their approach. They were probably aware of the timeline for the bombing run as well. Their eyes would be on the skies. Browne had just bought them five more minutes to finish up whatever they were doing and get clear.

If they're getting those hostages out, they'll have an extra few minutes on hand, he thought.

It wasn't much. But it was something.

Browne's eyes dropped to the clock.

Any minute now…

* * * * *

Shakira skidded to a stop at the edge of the mountain path overlooking the abandoned French base.

For the past few minutes, the skies had been filled with the sounds of gunfire and explosions. She had known that the American Jack Cody and her fiancé were walking into a battle. But she'd had no idea of its extent until now. It sounded like one of the major engagements she remembered from the war – a massive conflict between Afghan nationalist forces and the Taliban that had raged for hours and left hundreds dead in the valley near her village. She remembered having to stay home by herself as her aunt went to help those cleaning up and burying the bodies…

Tarak Khan is wisest and craftiest of all the hill bandits, she reminded herself. Her man had survived dozens of encounters with the enemy, whether Russian, American, Taliban or from Massoud's forces. Tarak Khan fought with the blessing of God upon him for his charity to the people. And if he died, it would be fighting the enemies of God. But Shakira felt confident he would not.

She crept to the edge of the path and peered over the edge at the base below.

Smoke crawled upwards from the blackened wreckage of tanks. Gunfire snapped and she saw the figures of men hurling themselves about, firing, running, seeking cover...

And there. *There!* She could see Khan's vehicle, the MRAP they had taken from American forces! She watched as the vehicle sped toward the center of the fighting.

CHAPTER 52

Cody, Watson, Showalter and McKnight regrouped, setting up a defensive position between two tanks and preparing to engage the enemy.

"We gotta get out of here!" Cody told Watson. "We've got minutes before this place goes up in smoke!"

"Roger that!" Watson cried, seizing up a fallen AK and racking its slide. "We cut our way clear and make for the main gate!"

Cody nodded. But inside, he was fighting a sinking feeling. Even if they gained the gate and made it outside the base, chances were, they'd be caught in the blast from the bomb run. Ordnance at that volume would suck every ounce of oxygen from the surrounding area and concentrate it in the final concussion. By his personal scale of reckoning, their likelihood of making it out alive diminished with each passing moment.

Time to focus on the objective, he thought. There was almost no chance of coming out of this thing in one piece. So Cody was determined to meet his objectives as best he could. He flicked a glance at Watson and her steely-eyed Marines. Death didn't bother them. They knew what was at stake, and they were not afraid. Their only objective now was to take as many of the enemy with them as they could.

A cry sounded from without, and a line of Talis rushed their position.

Cody threw the rifle to his shoulder and opened fire. How many of them were there? In the blur of violence and action, he could not tell. Because suddenly he and Watson's men were butchering them. Standing and snarling, Watson fired a long burst from her AK into the nearest enemy, one of whom was mere feet from her. Her salvo blasted him in half, the bullets sawing through him to cut down the man behind him.

McKnight and Showalter followed suit. Each one's AK bucked and chattered as they blasted round after round at Massoud's men. The first wave came charging, valiantly. And was mown down, valiantly. The second wave was strong but showed some hesitation. The two Marines exploited the half-second delay to put the fear of God into the charging Afghans. There was a pause before the third wave came.

They'll be conferring, Cody thought. And reached for a grenade.

"Here!" He handed grenades to Watson and her men. "Wait until the next explosion, then aim...*there.*" He pointed to an area near the parked vehicles where men seemed to be gathering.

Cody moved out from his position, flanking Massoud's position. Eyeballing it from the side, he saw that there was a way out – a narrow pathway leading to the main gate. He would get them out that way. Provided his plan worked. He had one set of explosives not yet detonated. He planned to do that now. *We'll at least have a fighting chance of getting clear before the bombing run starts!*

At that exact moment, the MRAP appeared. It braked to a halt by the gate. As Cody watched, the driver and passenger side doors opened and Tarak Khan and Shakira appeared, waving to them. *Come on!*

And suddenly there was a glimmer of hope.

* * * * *

Massoud paced back and forth, the scimitar in his fist. Who were these utter *fools* he had on his side? Fools and cowards, all!

"How is it the Americans are not yet defeated?"

"Soon, Great one! Soon!"

"There are only *three* of them!" Massoud thundered. "What is the *matter* with you? You number almost forty! And you cannot even d–"

An explosion rocked the compound. The sky had brightened sufficiently to reveal distinct shapes and types of vehicles. The first explosion was followed by a second and then a third close by.

More bombs! Massoud gritted his teeth. The saboteur had been thorough.

He remained upright until the next explosion. The force of the blast threw Massoud a short distance away. He shook his head and raised it, looking around.

Half his men lay spilled, their bodies torn by the shockwave. The other half were getting mowed down by the Marines.

That's when he saw the grenades falling toward them from the sky.

Cody watched as the line of Massoud's men crumpled under the blasts. Watson, Showalter and McKnight hurled their grenades. In the instant before the explosions, Cody cried out to them.

"This way!" He waved his rifle, pointing to the MRAP. *"MARINES! BUG OUT!"*

They didn't have to be told twice. As a unit, they wheeled and began sprinting for the gate, Cody in the lead. Watson brought up the rear. And with each passing step, the sky brightened toward dawn.

The bombers will be closing in on our position right now, he thought. If not for the MRAP, they would be sunk. But with Khan's sudden reappearance, there was a sudden sliver of hope gleaming like moonlight in darkness. Cody was going to be damned if he would let the chance pass without reaching for it with all he had.

They were barely two hundred yards from the gate when Massoud struck.

CHAPTER 53

High overhead, Browne's squadron was approaching the target area.

The radio crackled in Browne's headset. "Combat flight leader, this is Raptor 5. We have an open door. Repeat, we have an open door."

It was time. Browne's finger hit the transmit switch.

"Roger, Raptor 5. All birds, this is flight combat leader. Assume formation and commence bombing run."

CHAPTER 54

With a shout of challenge, Massoud leapt out suddenly in front of Watson from between two trucks, his sword slashing, blocking her off from the others.

"NOW YOU DIE!" Massoud shrieked, raising the sword above his head.

All the pent-up rage and humiliation he had experienced at their hands of these Americans, his schemes to enrich himself and his organization, his ultimate goal of assuming a place of honor among the Taliban – everything was crumbling to ash blown away in the wind.

These Americans would pay.

Starting with the bitch!

* * * * *

Cody spun at the sound of gunfire. A handful of Massoud's men were left and had decided to engage them from behind. Cody unloaded half a magazine at them. Showalter and McKnight did, too, firing until their weapons were empty.

Cody looked to the sky. And saw the dark shapes of planes etching the clouds.

They were here.

"COME ON!" he cried, firing one last burst into Massoud's men.

"The lieutenant!" McKnight made ready to turn back. *"She's –"*

Cody could see: Massoud had her cut off, menacing her with a sword. Cody raised his C8, sighted and squeezed the trigger.

CLICK!

Misfire! The weapon was overheated, its firing pin possibly bent from overuse. He threw it to the ground.

"LT!" screamed Showalter.

"SAVE YOURSELVES!" Watson cried. *"GET TO THE GATE! THAT'S AN ORDER!"*

"LT! No!" Desperation rang in McKnight's voice.

"I SAID GO!" She fixed her eyes on Cody. *"GET MY MEN TO SAFETY!"*

Cody hesitated. Then looked skyward again.

The bombers were coming! The airborne rumble of their approach began hammering the atmosphere.

Without another word, he gestured the Marines toward the MRAP waiting at the gate.

* * * * *

Watson knew she was dead. Yet she had never felt more alive in her entire life.

I'm actually going to get to kill that son of a bitch, she marveled.

The time had come.

The man with the sword swung it high over his head, ready to bring down on her in a thrusting, cutting motion. Powerful, but too slow. She evaded it easily. He almost caught her with the back slash, but she was outside its arc when it came. Watson held her breath, waiting for it to reach the end of its swing, then…

She struck.

Head down, shoulders rounded, she hit the man dead center with a football tackle. He went down, the sword clattering from his hands. And like the proud fool he was, he grasped at her, rolling on top, assuming his superior strength would save him.

Big mistake – one which numerous men had made when training with her.

Watson emptied her mind, focused her breath and inhabited the moment. Each breath was a second, each movement part of a flow. When Massoud reached for her neck, she intercepted the hand. Twisted. He roared as his fingers got bent back. Then she was sweeping him, coming up on top in the mount position. His astonishment showed plain on his face the second before she punched him. Her knuckles connected to his mouth with a satisfying *SMACK!*

Then she was slamming him again and again – hard shots, directly to the face. Her knuckles split and she kept punching until she felt the nose break with a bone-shattering *crunch*. Her next shot jarred teeth, moistening his beard with blood.

Suddenly strong with panic, Massoud managed to bridge up and partially dislodge her. But Watson wrapped her legs around his waist and maneuvered until she had his back. Her left arm snaked around his neck and her right moved in to grasp and pull the wrist, sinking the choke.

"This is for Davis," she whispered. "And Wendell."

Slowly, she cut off his blood and airflow. One moment he was thrashing. Then he had gone limp. When she reached the point where she would ordinarily release the choke, she bore down. With a final spasm, Abdul Massoud died fighting for breath in a torment of blood and snot.

She rose to her feet unsteadily.

Goddam it, I actually killed the son of a bitch! she thought. Then she turned and sprinted for the truck. She managed five steps before the bullet stopped her.

* * * * *

"LT!"

Cody saw the wounded Tali rise and snap off a shot. An instant later, Khan finished him with a burst from the MRAP's sixty-cal, but the damage was done. The bullet had shattered Watson's calf. She was lying in a pool of her own blood. But damn if she still wasn't trying to get to the MRAP.

Cody leaned out and shouted to Massoud: "Go! We'll catch up!" He jumped to the ground, ready to make a bid for Watson... when suddenly Shakira streaked past him and ran in through the gates of the base.

* * * * *

She was the Girl Who Ran.

Now more than ever, her talents were required. And she

didn't hesitate for a moment.

Shakira focused her eyes on the female marine lying inside the base gates. She had no idea what she would do once she got there. But the woman was wounded and needed an extra pair of legs to get clear before the bombers came. And Shakira's were the fastest around.

Her world became the joggling up-and-down view of the road, the smack of her heel strikes, the thunder of her breathing as it roared in her ears. She was screaming inside: *go, go, go!* First objective: make it to the fallen woman.

She skidded to a stop beside Watson.

"Who the hell are you?" Watson asked.

"My name is Shakira," she replied. "I've come to help you!"

"Help yourself and get clear! If those bombers arrive while we're still here..."

"Then at least you won't die alone!" Shakira bent, grasped Watson's arm with surprising strength and lifted her.

The Marine screamed in pain as she came to her feet. The girl looped an arm around her waist, shrugged her shoulders under so Watson could grip her. And, together, they started down the road toward the gate.

Shakira kept her eyes on the MRAP. *Go, go, go!* she told herself again. Watson was hopping on her good leg, dragging the wounded one behind her. Shakira did not look back at the trail of blood the woman left in their wake and did not turn when the drone of the bombers rose behind her.

Go, go, go!

The gate was there, an impossible distance ahead. Until...

Someone was coming toward her. Someone fast and strong. She didn't recognize Cody until he was on top of them.

"Come on!" He grappled Watson into a fireman's carry.

The first whistling shrieks of descending bombs cut the dawn glow.

The road...the gate...the roar of bombers overhead...

And then they were piling into the rear of the armored vehicle. The doors slammed and Tarak Khan floored the pedal to the metal.

CHAPTER 55

Two miles out from the base, Khan hit the brakes so they could all tumble out of the vehicle to watch the airstrike.

Watson needed assistance, wincing in pain. Cody and Shakira helped so she could view the spectacle of the F-35s swooping into rain down ordnance like the wrath of God on Massoud's base.

Explosions geysered, throwing up spumes of soil and sheets of flame. As the bombs detonated, vehicles and weapons flew skyward, shattering, adding to the chaos. A great rumbling shook the ground. Soon a black cloud of ash covered the base. Slowly, the squadron began walking the explosions down the length of the facility.

It continued this way for half-an-hour. And then?

Silence.

"In the name of Allah..." Tarak Khan shook his head in wonder. "Such power!"

"Yeah." Cody nodded. "I'd say that anyone who wants to

claim those weapons now is going to have to bring a shovel. And lots of glue."

His cellphone rang. Cody dragged it from a pocket and checked the caller ID.

Sara!

He smiled as he answered.

"Hey, stranger," he said. "I was starting to worry."

"The Talis crossed into Uzbekistan and hit our forward operating area," she said.

"You okay?" Cody glanced over his shoulder. He walked a short distance away from the MRAP to continue the call.

"I'll be okay. Bullet wound to the shoulder. I'm in an Uzbek military hospital now."

"I'm heading back that way. May take a while, though."

"You've got a chopper?"

"No, I've thumbed a ride. With some, ah, friends."

Sara laughed. "You'll have to tell me all about it when you get here. Listen… someone wants to talk to you."

"Who?"

"Stand by and I'll connect you."

Cody waited. Khan and his men were cheering and high fiving around the back of the MRAP. Just inside, Shakira and McKnight were bent over, tending Watson. The Marine lieutenant was obviously in pain, but the grin spreading across her features told him she'd be alright.

With a click, the call went through.

"Cody? You there?"

Recognizing the voice, Cody straightened. "Mr. President!

Hello."

"Glad to hear you're alright." Harwood laughed. "After action reports are coming in now. That base no longer exists. What about our people?"

"Three recovered, Mr. President. One wounded. But for the most part, none the worse for wear."

The President released a long-held sigh of relief. "Thank God," he said quietly. "I've been receiving intel both from the French and via drone. The ranking officer is a Lieutenant Watson. Is she among the...?"

"She's fine, Mr. President." Cody glanced back at the wounded Marine where she lay receiving treatment. "Wounded but alive."

"That's good, because..." Harwood hesitated. "She's shown unbelievable courage and leadership. I've conferred with the commandant of the Marine Corps, and he agrees. Her actions went above and beyond the call of duty. Her service will be properly recognized and rewarded. Once she recovers, Lieutenant Watson will be recommended for the Congressional Medal of Honor."

"Glad to hear that, sir," said Cody. "It's richly deserved."

"I figured you would agree," said the President. "There's, ah, someone else we should recognize. There's a girl in that village. Her name is Shakira. I'm told she personally provided intelligence to the French at great risk to herself?"

"Yes, sir. That's true. She's a truly remarkable person." Cody smiled. "I'm looking at her right now."

"So she's okay?"

"Yes, sir. She's doing fine."

"Good to hear." The President was quiet for a moment. "I'd like to speak to her if that's alright."

"Of course, sir."

* * * * *

At Cody's request, Shakira came and accepted the phone from him. She had spoken on a telephone once before so was familiar with the technology. As Cody walked a short distance off and sat down on a rock, she lifted the device to her ear.

"Hello?"

"Is this Shakira?"

"This is Shakira Naziri."

"Hello, Shakira. My name is Martin Harwood. I'm the President of the United States. And I'm very honored to meet you."

Shakira started. "Mr. President! The honor is mine. Sir, you will be pleased to hear that Abdul Massoud's base has been destroyed and your brave Marines recovered."

"Good!"

"Lieutenant Watson has been injured by a gunshot. But we are taking her to receive care. She will recover, I am quite sure. We Afghans know how to treat gunshot wounds, Mr. President. It's something we do very well."

"I bet. Shakira, I wanted to extend the thanks of a grateful nation. America is indebted to you for your courage, your sacrifice and your service in our cause. As we are to all the Afghan people who helped and supported us while we were in your country. We did not wish to leave you, but we had no choice. And we will continue to support the efforts of Afghan people seeking freedom."

"Thank you, Mr. President."

"I understand you're a runner."

She blushed. "Yes, Mr. President. I love to run."

"Well, the women's track team at UC Berkeley is one of the finest in the country. Perhaps in the entire world. I have spoken to their coach. Shakira, there is a place for you on their squad. And as a student at the university. We would like to invite you to come to the United States. It would be a great honor to offer you citizenship. America needs people like you."

Shakira absorbed all of this in wordless silence. A tremor shook her deep inside. It was a combination of many feelings: gratitude, wonder, humility. She picked her way calmly through these emotions with care until she found her calmness. With a breath to steady herself, she replied.

"Mr. President, that is a generous and wonderful offer. America is a great, *great* country. I am honored to call you friends. I thank you... But I must refuse your kind offer."

She noted Cody perk up and turn to her when she said this.

"As much as I would love to visit America and meet the women runners of whom you speak, my place is here." She waved a hand to encompass the desert, the nation. "I am engaged to be married to the most *wonderful* man! A strong man. A great leader, like yourself. He is considered an outlaw by the Taliban, but his heart is honorable and good. He is valiant and strong, and he serves the poor. I want to stand by his side, Mr.

President. I want to help him fight for freedom and serve the people. I want to give him babies that we can raise and teach so that they in turn can take up the fight and continue it after we're gone. Most of all, sir, I want to stay and care for my village. You see, I have a very important job."

Harwood considered this. "What is your job, Shakira?" he asked.

"I am the fastest runner. Faster than any man. If the village encounters trouble, I am to run and seek help. If I leave, who will do this? There is no one else. It is a responsibility I accept. Many people are depending on me, sir."

Harwood sat stunned for a long moment. Then he laughed. "I...don't know what to say to that. Except that your village, and your fiancé, are very, very lucky indeed. Alright, then. I understand. God bless you, Shakira."

"And you, Mr. President."

* * * * *

For a long time after Shakira hung up and they resumed their journey, Cody sat silently in the passenger seat of the MRAP, watching Afghanistan float past outside his window.

"Your fiancée just got off the phone with the President," he said to Khan. "He invited her to emigrate to America. She, uh, turned him down."

Behind the wheel, Khan poked out his lower lip and nodded, as if Shakira's choice had been the obvious one.

"Is good decision. Shakira knows where her duty lies. It is

with her husband, her village, our people."

"Tarak...if someone offered you a million dollars and the chance to leave the country, would you?"

"No, Jack Cody. I love money. And I am starting to like America, almost a little bit. But what good is a million dollars if I cannot share it with my people? No. Shakira shows good sense. I have chosen well."

"You have," said Cody. He drew in his breath to add something, then paused.

There was nothing left to say. Nothing at all.

For now: mission accomplished.

A LOOK AT: SAY IT WAS MURDER
BY STEPHEN MERTZ

CRITICALLY ACCLAIMED AUTHOR STEPHEN MERTZ IS BACK WITH A PRIVATE EYE NOVEL—CRACKLING WITH PLOT TWISTS AND ENDLESS SUSPENSE.

McShan is tough and smart—a top operative for the detective agency Honeycutt Personal Services. But when he's sent to the picturesque desert landscape of southeastern Arizona to check on the well-being of a former Olympic gymnast who's become involved with a New Age cult, his hands are suddenly full.

It doesn't take long for murder to rear its ugly head, and McShan finds himself neck-deep in a case involving vicious bikers, an unassuming barber who may be a criminal mastermind, a wealthy entrepreneur hiding dangerous secrets, and too many beautiful blondes with deadly secrets of their own.

Populated with compelling characters and told with a sharp, contemporary edge, this private eye classic will leave readers everywhere breathless.

"Stephen Mertz is the best action writer I've read in a long time!" —Brent Towns

COMING JUNE 2022

ABOUT THE AUTHOR

Stephen Mertz is an American fiction author who is best known for his mainstream thrillers and novels of suspense. His work covers a wide variety of styles from paranormal dark suspense (Night Wind and Devil Creek) to historical speculative thrillers (Blood Red Sun) and hardboiled noir (Fade to Tomorrow). Mertz is also a popular lecturer on the craft of writing and has appeared as a guest speaker before writer's groups and at universities.

During high school and college, Steve regularly scandalized his "literary, well-intentioned" creative writing teachers with "thud and blunder melodramas." Throughout military service, travel, and a wide variety of jobs, his goal remained to become a publishing, full-time freelance professional. "It was never a question for me of if, but always when." His first national sale was to a mystery magazine, and his first novel, a detective thriller entitled Some Die Hard, was published under the pseudonym of Stephen Brett. Another Brett novel followed, as did a string of mystery and suspense short stories.

Steve's writing output increased dramatically when he emerged as one of the country's most in-demand writers of adventure paperback novels, averaging four books per year for ten years. His work on Don Pendleton's Mack Bolan series is regarded by fans as some of the best in that series. He also created the Mark Stone: MIA Hunter and Cody's Army series, written under the pseudonyms Jack Buchanan and Jim Case respectively.

Stephen Mertz has traveled widely and is a U.S. Army veteran. He presently lives in the American Southwest, and he is always at work on a new book.

CPSIA information can be obtained
at www.ICGtesting.com
Printed in the USA
LVHW091231280422
717465LV00007B/326